PEACE REBEL

Books by Robert Elmer

Adventures Down Under

#1 / *Escape to Murray River*
#2 / *Captive at Kangaroo Springs*
#3 / *Rescue at Boomerang Bend*
#4 / *Dingo Creek Challenge*
#5 / *Race to Wallaby Bay*
#6 / *Firestorm at Kookaburra Station*
#7 / *Koala Beach Outbreak*
#8 / *Panic at Emu Flat*

The Young Underground

#1 / *A Way Through the Sea*
#2 / *Beyond the River*
#3 / *Into the Flames*
#4 / *Far From the Storm*
#5 / *Chasing the Wind*
#6 / *A Light in the Castle*
#7 / *Follow the Star*
#8 / *Touch the Sky*

Promise of Zion

#1 / *Promise Breaker*
#2 / *Peace Rebel*

00B

ROBERT ELMER

BETHANY HOUSE PUBLISHERS
MINNEAPOLIS, MINNESOTA 55438

Cover illustration by Chris Ellison
Cover and page design by Lookout Design Group, Inc.
Typesetting by Aaron Sharar Design

Scripture quotations are from the King James Version of the Bible.

Published by Bethany House Publishers
A Ministry of Bethany Fellowship International
11400 Hampshire Avenue South
Minneapolis, Minnesota 55438
www.bethanyhouse.com

Printed in the United States of America by
Bethany Press International, Minneapolis, Minnesota 55438

Library of Congress Cataloging-in-Publication Data

Elmer, Robert.
Peace rebel / by Robert Elmer.
p. cm.— (Promise of Zion ; 2)
Summary: After escaping from a Jewish refugee ship, Dov, a Polish Jew, and Emily, the daughter of a British major, are taken to a Jewish kibbutz and are caught up in the danger and violence between the Jews, Arabs, and British in Palestine in 1947.
ISBN 0-7642-2297-X (pbk.)
1. Palestine—History—1917-1948—Juvenile fiction. [1. Palestine—History—1917-1948—Fiction. 2. Jews—Palestine.] I. Title.
PZ7.E4794 Pe 2000
[Fic]—dc21

99-051015
CIP

To Norm —

These things I have spoken unto you, that in me ye might have peace. In the world ye shall have tribulation: but be of good cheer; I have overcome the world.

—John 16:33

Robert Elmer is the author of several other series for young readers, including ADVENTURES DOWN UNDER and THE YOUNG UNDERGROUND. He got his writing start as a newspaper reporter but has written everything from magazine columns to radio and TV commercials. Now he writes full-time from his home in rural northwest Washington state, where he lives with his wife, Ronda, and their three busy teenagers.

CONTENTS

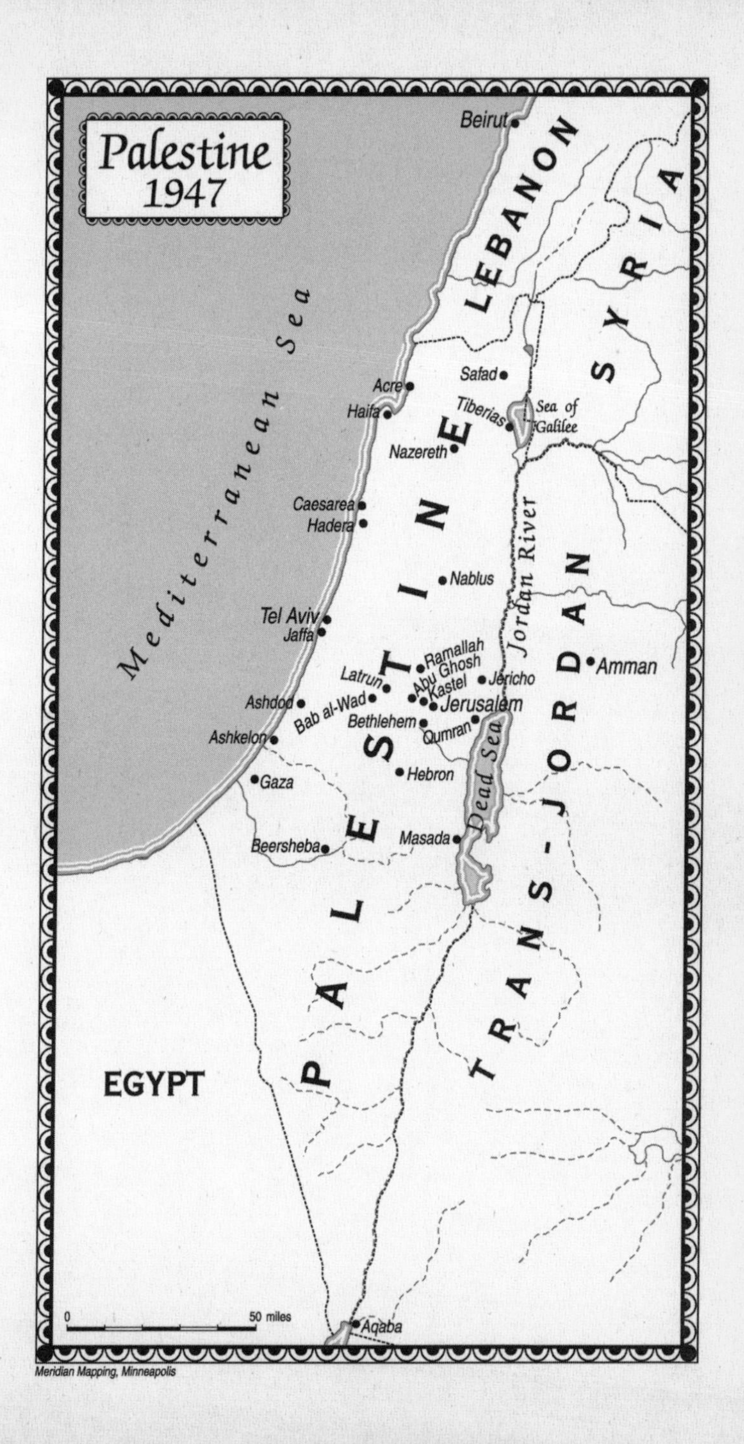
Palestine
1947
Beirut
LEBANON
SYRIA
Mediterranean Sea
Safad
Acre
Haifa
Tiberias
Sea of Galilee
Nazereth
Caesarea
Hadera
Nablus
Jordan River
Tel Aviv
Jaffa
Ramallah
Abu Ghosh
Latrun
Kastel
Jericho
Amman
Ashdod
Bab al-Wad
Jerusalem
Bethlehem
Qumran
Ashkelon
Hebron
Gaza
Dead Sea
Masada
Beersheba
PALESTINE
TRANS-JORDAN
EGYPT
0
50 miles
Aqaba
Meridian Mapping, Minneapolis

BIG MISTAKE

Palestine
September 1947

Dov dug his fingers into the sand and drew in a deep breath. After all these years, he'd finally made it to *Eretz Israel.* The land of Zion.

But this nighttime homecoming wasn't how he'd thought it would be—pushed overboard by a panicked crowd, then dragged through the warm Mediterranean waves to the beach, past the shouts and shots of British soldiers. One look at the *Aliyah 1947* told him the refugee transport was still floating—just barely—after it had been rammed in the side by one of the British destroyers. A ring of three battle-gray warships now surrounded the splintered vessel while the flashes of light and shots offshore told him the other Jews on board were still prisoners. Nineteen forty-seven was not a good year for Jews coming to Palestine.

No, it wasn't supposed to be like this. *And I wasn't supposed to get here alone.*

Dov's mother, *Imma*, had always told him they would go to Palestine someday, but then war had come to Poland, and everything had gone very wrong. Had Dov left his family behind in the ashes of Poland's death camps? Had he survived only to be alone?

Dov still held to a fragile hope. He had to. It was what had sent him searching for Imma and his father, *Abba*. His brother, Natan, too. And now that hope had washed up with him on the dark beach, where he sat and cried, alone.

Well, not completely alone. He only *felt* alone. The English girl still sat next to him, dripping wet, catching her breath. She was the daughter of the British major who had boarded the *Aliyah* to look for terrorists and try to keep the illegal Jewish refugees from coming to Palestine. The girl who, truthfully, had been his guardian angel. She'd saved him after she had been pushed off the ship, too—dragging to safety a wiry, dark-haired thirteen-year-old boy who could not swim.

Never mind that she'd had to punch him in the eye to keep him from drowning both of them. The eye still hurt, and he hoped it didn't look as bad as it felt.

"It's late and I shan't be staying here," announced the girl in English as she stood up. "I'm going to find my father."

The girl tried to straighten her soaked dress, but she still looked awful in the glow of the ship searchlights that flickered across the beach. She was wet, matted, and covered with sand, like a sugar-coated English pastry.

She was everything Dov was *not:* tall, straight-backed, pale skinned. She held her chin out like a princess even though she looked like a beggar.

Dov pushed his hands deeper into the sand, feeling the coolness. He didn't want to let go of the land, now that he had it in his hands. He had come so far to claim it.

"I don't know who you are." The girl broke into his thoughts. "But since you came off that awful ship, I'm certain people will think you don't belong here."

Don't belong here? The words almost seemed funny. Who *did* this girl think belonged in Palestine, if not a Jew? He heard a whistle off in the distance, this time from the land behind them.

The girl crossed her arms and shivered. "It's rather nippy out here."

Maybe so, he thought. But he wasn't going to let her see *him* shiver.

"You'll be all right," the girl continued, not seeming to care that Dov never said anything in return. "My father will see to it that you're treated fairly."

Dov thought she sounded like all the English he had ever met, like Miss Alexander back in the displaced persons camp. Quite in charge. Quite correct.

"Fairly?" Dov threw a handful of sand into the waves and answered her in English. "Do you call *that* fair?"

He meant what was happening to the *Aliyah* and its passengers, and she had to know it. They'd been chased, rammed, and now captured, all because they wanted to come to Eretz Israel. After all his people had been through during the war in Europe, how dare she say what was fair!

The English girl took a step backward, away from the water and toward the low sand dunes that framed the beach. The whistle sounded again, this time much closer. And as she turned away from the beach, she suddenly stood face-to-face with a dark shape, a bearded man dressed in black pants and a black shirt.

"Hurry," whispered the man in Hebrew. "There's no time. Follow me."

Emily gasped in fright and stared at the dark shadow of a man standing just inches from her. Try as she would, she could not move her legs to run or to follow. Her mouth went dry, and she couldn't stop her knees from shaking.

"I said, come!" the man whispered once more. "They'll be here any minute." He grabbed Emily's arm, half dragging her through the sand.

"No, wait," she started to say. Who "they" would be, at first Emily hadn't the foggiest idea. All she knew was that her father should have been here by now, and this was surely not her father, or anyone else under his command. Behind her, the ungrateful Jewish boy she had saved was dragged along by another shadowy figure. Perhaps *he* knew what was going on.

"I'm Emily Parkinson," she started to say. "And my father—"

"Introductions later," grunted the man, this time in rough English. He froze and turned his head to the side, listening to the night. Emily tried again.

"If you please, my father—"

He clapped a meaty hand over her mouth as they began to run. Or rather, *he* ran, his strong arm fixed around Emily in a near choke hold. Emily tried to scream, but no sound escaped the man's grip. Her legs flailed in a kick that connected only with the sand.

A whistle blew just over the sand dune to their left, causing the man to veer right. It was loud and shrill, the kind of whistle a policeman would blow to get someone to stop. Emily thought she heard men shouting. Surely *they* would be her father's men, would they not? But nothing halted her captor as he bounded through the dunes.

"Wait!" Emily cried the moment he relaxed his grip. She tried to hold her ground, but he pushed her into a low, protected spot. The dunes were behind them now.

As if it had been waiting for them, a delivery lorry backed quietly out of the shelter of a low cluster of bushes, its lights off. The back doors swung open.

"No!" insisted Emily, digging in her heels. "You don't understand!"

Why wouldn't this awful man listen to her? Who was he? She made one last desperate effort to turn around, to get away, but the man was too strong for her. He simply hoisted her sideways, one arm around her waist, nearly rolling her into the back of the delivery lorry.

"In you go, girl. Welcome to Eretz Israel."

The Jewish boy came tumbling in right behind her; then the doors slammed shut and a latch was rammed into place. Outside, someone hit the back of the vehicle twice, and the driver gunned the motor before lurching away.

What in the world? Only a few hours before, Emily had been standing on the Jewish refugee ship, safely within the sight of her army officer father. But then the passengers had panicked and the railing had snapped, sending her and this boy into the dark ocean. She could scarcely believe how quickly things had turned bad. She recalled the British guards shooting into the water, and her narrow escape. *Quite horrible to think, but I could have been shot by Father's own men!* The shooting was all a mistake, of course—not at all her father's fault. None of the soldiers had known quite what to do in that awful riot. They were only doing their job; it was understandable.

Emily closed her eyes and the tears came. Understandable?

For a minute back there on the beach—but only a short minute—she thought she had done the right thing by dragging the boy to shore with her. She'd *thought* it was the proper English thing, even the Christian thing to do. If it *had* been the right thing, though, she wouldn't have been dragged into this horrid lorry and thrown about as if she were a sack of potatoes, for goodness' sake! The cramped space smelled of petrol fumes, grease, and wet people.

"You've made a horrible mistake!" Emily pounded on the back door. "I'm not one of them! Don't you understand? I'm Emily Parkinson, and my father is Major Parkinson!"

Emily kept pounding, scraping her knuckles raw on a latch she couldn't see.

"You'd better sit down, Emily Parkinson" came an older man's voice from the darkness behind her.

Emily was not about to take advice from whoever might be locked in the darkness with her. What mattered now was reaching the driver and stopping him before they traveled any farther.

Emily turned toward the front of the vehicle. She couldn't see a window, but perhaps it was just too dark outside to tell the difference. She tried to find a way forward but stumbled over wet, shivering bodies.

"Oh!" Emily cried, and she tried to get to her feet. "Terribly sorry." But the truck squealed around a corner, sending everyone rolling. A pipe or something metal rolled across the floor and clanged against the wall.

"As I said, Emily Parkinson, you'd better sit down." It was the same man's voice, in English with a thick Yiddish accent.

Emily found a spot on the floor that wasn't taken. What did it matter if she sat on the floor? Her dress was ruined anyway. But she could hardly keep from bursting out in sobs. Surely this was a nightmare, and she would wake up in a moment to find herself safely tucked away in her own bed in the large, comfortable home she shared with her mother and father in the fashionable Rehavia district of Jerusalem. Ginger, her maid, would be there with a lovely plate of chocolate cakes and good, strong tea sweetened with two sugar cubes, maybe three, and a dollop of milk.

"Are you and the boy together?" A voice from inside the dark lorry interrupted her tea party. "From the ship, also, of course?"

"No!" snapped Emily, growing more and more irritated at the nightmare. "There's been a terrible mix-up. I don't belong here, you see, and—"

Emily couldn't finish as the lorry swerved wildly around a corner, then picked up speed.

✡ ✡ ✡

It didn't matter how hard Emily Parkinson pounded on the side of the truck; the driver never let them out. Starting and stopping, turning and bumping—who knew how long they had driven into the night? Dov sat quietly, wondering how he had ever gotten mixed up with the British officer's daughter.

The others sat quietly, too, lost in their own thoughts. He figured about ten others from the *Aliyah* had made it into the truck. A few in the corner hummed Jewish songs as they bumped along. They were, after all, finally in Zion. It just wasn't the kind of welcome any of them had imagined.

Several times Dov thought he heard shots outside. One of the others said they were only the sounds of a car as it backfired, but Dov knew better. He'd heard enough shots during the war. So had everyone else, he guessed. Except perhaps for the major's nervous daughter. But even she grew silent after a while.

Someone started coughing in the corner. Someone else was crying. The singers hummed a little louder, maybe to cover the noise. Suddenly they screeched to a halt.

"This is it!" someone announced. They rose to their feet, shoulder to shoulder, sardines in a tin. By this time Dov might have preferred the smell of sardines to that of the closed-in truck.

Again they heard muffled voices outside, but Dov couldn't understand a word of what was being said. Someone yelled. A shot, then something hard hit the side of the truck, then another. The driver's door slammed. More shouting.

"What's going on?" asked Dov.

MIDNIGHT AMBUSH

2

"I don't care what's going on," Emily Parkinson said. "I'm getting out of here." She stood and pounded on the back door.

"I say!" she cried. "We're still shut in here. I demand to be let out this instant."

Now she's demanding, thought Dov. *That's—*

He didn't have time to finish his thought as one of the twin doors was yanked open.

"Hallo …?" Emily suddenly didn't sound quite so brave.

Everyone held still, waiting to see who moved first. Only Emily slid forward and balanced on the lip of the truck as if ready to jump down, not waiting for anyone to help her.

"Can you tell me where we are?" she called out to the crowd that had pressed in around them. Burning torches lit their dark faces. No one was smiling.

Emily seemed unconcerned. "I need a telephone right away," she told them, holding a pretend phone to her ear. "To ring up my father."

Instead of answering, a man at the back of the crowd raised a fist and, in a language Dov didn't recognize, yelled what must have been an unkind comment. A few more raised their own fists in response.

Emily backed up, blinking. "Oh dear. You needn't get so upset."

"Oh dear" was right. As far as Dov could see, this was no welcoming committee, and far worse than what they had met back on the beach. A quick glance told him they were surrounded by squat, stone-block houses on a narrow lane in the middle of an Arab village. But why were there so many people in the streets at this time of night?

Maybe the truck driver hadn't expected the crowd, either. In any case, this was obviously not a good place to stop with a load of Jewish refugees coming to settle the Promised Land. The truck shook as some of the mob began pushing it from side to side.

"What's happening out there?" squeaked a frightened woman behind Dov. She had found a hiding place in a dark corner of the truck as far away as possible from the open doors. "Why are they pushing us? We don't have anything to give them."

Perhaps not, but the truck must have been too much of an attraction for the late-night crowd to ignore. What sounded like a piece of metal was twisted off the outside. A mirror, probably. Were they a wreck to be stripped, the cargo inside carried away?

One of the young men in the crowd reached in and grabbed the nearest ankle. It happened to be Dov's.

"*Nain!* No!" Dov slipped into Yiddish as he kicked the grip free. Somehow they would have to close the doors again, but the handles were on the outside. From this side all they had to grip was a narrow bar and small latch. He leaned out and reached for it.

"Watch out!" warned Emily, grabbing his shoulder. "You'll

fall."

What did she know? A minute before, she had been asking for a telephone from this bunch.

Dov grabbed for the latch just as their driver started the truck's motor once again, blasting the horn.

"Wait!" Dov gripped the inside latch with his fingers. When the truck inched ahead, the doors swung still wider, carrying Dov with them.

"Whoaaa!" Dov did his best to anchor his toes on the ledge behind him. But unless he wanted to let go and fall into the fist-shaking crowd that was running after them, he had to hold on to the door.

So he hung there on the open door, hoping not to fall as someone grabbed for his pant leg and the truck rattled on ahead, picking up speed.

I can't hold on. Dov was sure he would be the mob's first victim. His sweaty grip began to slip.

But just then the truck jerked to a stop, and as fast as the doors had been forced open, they swung shut with a *slam!* Dov toppled inside.

"Hold the door closed," he told the others who moved forward to help. Once again, they jolted and bumped their way down the gravel road.

✡ ✡ ✡

The road seemed to grow worse once they left the village, and for the next half hour they took turns holding the door shut, peeking out at the darkness every once in a while. No one knew where they were going. Dov tried to wedge himself against the wall where he could stay clear of the English girl. Despite what she had done for him, he didn't trust her any more than he trusted anyone else. Maybe he could find a way to escape these people. All of them.

"I was hoping they would take us to Tel Aviv," said a woman in Yiddish, the language most of the passengers spoke. "It's the easiest place to get a job."

"No, no, no," argued a man. "We're going up to Jerusalem, I'm sure. It's the only place for a Jew to live."

"But Tel Aviv—"

"Woman, I tell you I'm right—Jerusalem." The man was sounding more and more obnoxious. That's what happened after an hour or two in a dark box, not to mention everything before that on the *Aliyah*. Jerusalem, Tel Aviv, Jerusalem. Who really cared?

Actually, Dov hoped the man was right. He thought about where his parents might have gone, if they had somehow made it to Jerusalem, too. It had been so long. How would he ever find them? How would they even recognize him, or he them?

Don't think like that! Dov scolded himself and tried to think of something else. The handful of singers in the front of the truck had resumed their nonstop humming, sometimes louder, sometimes softer.

"Could we have some quiet for a change?" groused the man who was on his way to Jerusalem. "Here we are in this stinking box, and all you can do is…*sing*. Why—"

"We've stopped again!" The woman nearest Dov announced the obvious. They heard voices outside, a chain jingling, and a shout before they resumed bumping their way down yet another road. This time the trip lasted just a few minutes, and they stopped again.

"We're here!" cried the Jerusalem man. "The Holy City!"

✡ ✡ ✡

If they *had* arrived in Jerusalem, the Holy City was quite a lot quieter than Emily remembered. True, the sun wouldn't be up for a few more hours. But Emily was used to hearing the pre-dawn noise of the city—the exhaust-belching lorries rumbling down the streets, the dogs barking, the clattering of carts making their early morning rounds.

All she heard here after the engine shut down was quiet, then the creaking of the doors as their driver came around to let them out. Emily didn't try to count her sore spots from the long, bumpy ride. It felt as if they had driven around the entire countryside of Palestine.

Outside, the cooing sound of a pair of mourning doves told Emily they weren't in Jerusalem or Tel Aviv. This wasn't even a city. She straightened her sore back and slipped out of the lorry with the rest of the passengers.

"Welcome to Kibbutz Yad Shalom," announced a boy only a few years older than she was. Fifteen or sixteen, she guessed, though he looked as athletic as a professional soccer player. The glow from the flashlight he held lit up his sharp features, which were framed by a neat crop of jet-black hair. "My name is Henrik Melchior."

"Where's Ruben?" asked the driver in American-accented English, waving his hands in obvious frustration.

"I'm sorry," said their host. "The kibbutz leaders aren't here, and no one told us when you'd be arriving. Everyone else was tired from the harvest, so they went to bed early, which leaves me and the guard at the gate."

Henrik's English made him sound Scandinavian to Emily, though he didn't look it. But he was friendly, in any case—the first friendly face she had seen in many hours. His cheek-to-cheek smile was enough to light up the darkness.

"But—" the man who had hoped to go to Jerusalem sputtered as he looked around at the dark outlines of small farm buildings and the low hills surrounding them on three sides. "We thought we would be taken to Jerusalem!"

A strange mix of Yiddish and English, this.

"Or Tel Aviv," added the woman from the corner.

"Oh, if that's where you're wanting to go," said Henrik, "I'm sure you'll be able to get there eventually, but this farm is your first stop. Tel Aviv is a few miles north of us. Perhaps you've already noticed it's a bit difficult to travel."

"Difficult is right." Their driver cleared his throat. He thumped the side of his vehicle, looking for dents in between the *Wassermann & Sons, Plumbers* lettering. "From the beach by Caesarea, we circled around Tel Aviv to get here without being stopped; then we had to circle around every Arab town in Palestine, every roadblock. The one town I thought would be quiet was where we found trouble."

"You had trouble?" Henrik lowered his eyes. "We were afraid of that. My mother and I prayed."

"Not hard enough," grumbled the driver, slamming the back doors of his lorry as he returned to climb back into the driver's seat. "I stopped for an old man in the middle of the road, and just like that"—he snapped his fingers—"we were surrounded. They would have pulled the wheels right off the truck if I hadn't been able to get going again."

"I'm sorry to hear that." Henrik looked at the lorry. "It's good that you and these people are safe, though. The truck still runs, doesn't it?"

"Humph." The driver wasn't satisfied. "They don't pay me enough for this headache. If it's not the Arabs, it's the British. Everyone's against us! You tell whoever wants to know that I'm not making the trip again for a long time. Not again—not until the roads are clear. And who knows when that will be."

Henrik nodded seriously while their driver started up the lorry with a roar.

"Excuse me, sir." Emily rapped politely on the door of the lorry and looked up at the window.

The driver rolled his eyes up and the window down.

She swallowed hard and told herself the man would help once he understood who she was. He had to. "Excuse me, but I *obviously* don't belong with these people. You see, my father is Major Parkinson, and—"

"Tell your problems to the people here at the kibbutz." The driver interrupted her with an impatient wave of his hand. "They're the ones who want to help. Not me."

"Yes, but I need to get home to Jerusalem immediately. There's been a terrible mistake and—"

"Are you taking us to Jerusalem?" The man who had been so annoying during the trip hurried around the corner. He must have overheard Emily's question.

"Oy!" The driver hit his forehead with the palm of his hand, shoved the gearshift handle with a mighty grinding sound, and jerked forward. "No more rides, no more passengers! I've been driving three days now, and the roads get worse every day."

"But my father can pay you. . . ." Emily tried one last time, but her words were drowned out in the roar of the engine.

RUDE AWAKENING

Emily stomped her foot into the dusty road and stared at the disappearing delivery vehicle, but there was nothing she could do. For tonight, she would have to stay at the kibbutz.

"Tomorrow is going to be a big day here on the kibbutz." Henrik was at her side. "Perhaps you'd like to rest a bit before everyone else wakes up. Sleep, if you can."

Sleep, thought Emily, and the mention of the word turned her eyelids heavy. *A little sleep would be quite heavenly, in a real bed that doesn't bounce like a lorry on a dusty road.*

✡ ✡ ✡

When Emily awoke the next morning, she had no idea where she was or how she got there. Her back rebelled against the hard cot under her, and the rough, olive-colored wool army blanket felt much scratchier than her soft cotton sheets at home. And what was that horrible noise?

"La-la, la-la-la, la-la!" It sounded as if every Jewish person in Palestine had gathered to sing a chorus outside her window.

Emily sat up and tried to rub away the headache that had hit her like a brick between the eyes. The sun streaming past the sheet hung in front of the glassless window didn't help any.

What was the name of this kibbutz, this Jewish farm where dozens of families lived together? Something about peace—in Hebrew, *shalom*. Kibbutz Yad Shalom. *Monument to peace*. But at this time in the morning, with the earsplitting singing outside and the clapping in time to the music of a mandolin, well, it didn't sound at all peaceful.

At least no one else was in the room, which looked like some kind of bunkhouse. Rough cots, about twenty of them, lined the wall. Above each neatly made bed, a simple wooden shelf held a cup, a comb, a flower or two, and sometimes a small leather or cloth bag. She could tell the things belonged to girls, or women perhaps. But she also imagined this was what an army sleeping barracks might look like.

"La-la …" The music and the clapping grew even louder. Emily slipped out of bed and looked for her clothes. She didn't remember who had given her the long flannel nightgown she was wearing. Someone in the cot next to her? Her mind felt confused, and nearly everything from the night before was a blur: the commotion at the *Aliyah*, the long lorry ride, arriving at Yad Shalom, finding an extra bed, and now … What time was it?

Emily's growling stomach gave her a clue; she couldn't remember eating a full meal since she had been with her parents, and that was surely a long time ago. Since then she'd only been able to grab a few hurried bites, nothing more. Emily seemed to remember someone giving her a piece of fruit, a banana perhaps, just before she fell asleep. It was gone, though; she must have eaten it.

The scent of something cooking told her to get up. She

dressed quickly in the handmade skirt and blouse someone had laid out next to her cot, then hurried out into the sunshine.

✡ ✡ ✡

Dov tried to pull a pillow over his head to block out the morning noise, but the singers sounded as if they had started one of their *hora* dances right there in the middle of his army tent. He didn't have to see them to imagine them: They would be holding hands in a circle, another smaller circle inside the first, and the two groups would be moving in opposite directions. People had tried to do this dance on the ship, but there hadn't been quite enough room on deck, so the circles had turned into jagged, kidney-bean-shaped jumbles.

Here, though, they were singing "la-la" to the dance music at the top of their lungs. "La-la" because if the Jews on this kibbutz were anything like the Jews on the ship coming from Europe, they each spoke two or three languages—and usually not the same ones. Some German, or Polish, or Russian, or French. A bit of Yiddish, a little English and Hebrew. In this new land, getting everyone to sing in the same tongue was going to be as challenging as trying to carry on a conversation. "La-la" would have to do for now.

"Ohhh," Dov groaned and wondered what time it was. Surely the people in this kibbutz didn't dance every day at dawn, did they? If so, they were crazier than he already thought.

But when Dov opened his eyes again, he realized it was well past dawn. With the golden sun almost straight overhead, it had to be closer to midmorning, or later. And before his eyes could focus, he knew that someone was staring in at him, into the tent. He shook his head of the cobwebs and peeked out through his tent flap.

"Is somebody there?" Dov cleared the frog from his throat and rubbed his eyes.

Everyone was there. Across a dusty sort of plaza, the kibbutz farmers had clustered maybe a dozen tents and half that number again of wooden shacks. One, the only proper-looking building, had a canvas roof stretched over the main door for shade. Most of the kibbutz families had found a place there to watch the fun, but there were nearly as many people singing and dancing and in the parade as there were watching.

Dov caught sight of Emily stumbling out of one of the shedlike buildings directly across from his tent. Like him, she stared at the odd sight.

If this was truly a parade, it was definitely Hebrew in style, led by the hora dancers, twirling in circles and raising plenty of dust to go around. Behind them came young children leading their skinny black-and-white goats, which were finely combed and wearing bright ribbons in their ears. Most of the goats were busy chewing off their decorations, but no one seemed to care.

Next followed a few adults carrying bundles of grain and hopping in time to the music.

"The singers from the truck ride are going to feel right at home here," mumbled Dov as he shuffled out to get a better look. He still hadn't shaken the feeling that someone was watching him. Probably the same person who had been peeking into his tent when he was just waking up.

From around the corner of one of the sheds came the older boy who had first met them last night. Henrik. Henrik Melchior, he had told them when they'd first arrived. That was it.

Or rather, Dov *thought* it was him. Henrik led a crew of young children, each carrying a dusty red chicken. Henrik himself wore a floppy red paper decoration on his head.

What in the world?

"Kooey-kel-ee-koooeey!" The costume finally made sense when Henrik threw back his head and did his best rooster imitation.

"There you are!" cried Henrik.

Dov tried to look away, but Henrik changed course to greet him.

"I was afraid you might sleep through the whole *Hag Habikurim* festival," said Henrik as a noisy bunch of singers walked by.

"Pardon?" Dov tried to look as if he talked to roosters every day.

"The 'Feast of the Firstfruits' festival." Henrik handed his squawking chicken to a younger boy next to him. "It's a festival outlined in the book of Exodus, and—"

"Sure, I know it," Dov interrupted. "We celebrated it all the time in between forced labor at the Czestochowa munitions plant. At the death camp, too."

The older boy stopped for a moment and looked at Dov. "I know you've been through a lot more than I have. I'm sorry."

Dov sighed. "Don't be. Just tell me how to get out of this crazy place."

But Henrik obviously wasn't going to give up yet. "The war was hard in Denmark, but I never lived through anything like a…er, concentration camp."

"I told you not to feel sorry for me. You made it through the war, and so did I. And now I don't want to talk about it."

Dov saw the hurt look on Henrik's face, but he wasn't about to take back his harsh words. He glanced around at the stark, sandy hills that surrounded them. Where were all the trees? Why was everyone so happy in this barren place?

Happy, perhaps, but when he looked around, he could find

things that reminded him of the terrible Nazi death camps. A guard tower, complete with a guard holding a rifle, stood watch in a far corner of the property, and a barbed-wire fence surrounded the edges. A gate with a gatekeeper. Why all the fuss?

Henrik followed the direction of Dov's gaze.

"The barbed wire and everything are needed because we're surrounded by Arab villages here on the coast. Sometimes, well...maybe we can talk about that later. That's my mother over there."

He pointed out a petite woman on the edge of the crowd. Except for her height, she looked a lot like her son—dark haired, attractive, with sharp features. She smiled and waved.

"Let me show you around," Henrik said. "Introduce you. There are a hundred and ten of us, I think. About thirty kids. Even us kids work, although we have school, too. We all work together, raising chickens for eggs, keeping cows for beef and cheese—we sell that—and growing things like wheat and ..."

Dov shrugged as Henrik explained about their crops. If Henrik wanted to show him around, he supposed that was all right with him, as long as their tour took them to the place where the good food smells were coming from.

"Pardon me." Emily had discovered them talking—or rather, Henrik talking.

"Good morning!" boomed Henrik. His smile was back in full force. "Or perhaps I should say good afternoon? I'm supposed to show you two around, but I don't even know your names."

"Mine's Emily Parkinson." Emily nodded politely as she looked around. "And I shall need you to show me to your telephone immediately, please. I must contact my parents. You see, I was brought here by mistake and ..."

Emily's voice dropped off. "Why does he have to stare so?"

"Was I staring?" Henrik held up his hands innocently. "Pardon, I didn't mean to—"

"No, not you." Emily pointed over Henrik's shoulder. "That large fellow over there behind that shed."

DEADLY FIND

4

Dov guessed without looking what Emily was pointing at. It had to be the same person who had been staring at him when he first woke.

"He's gone now." Emily frowned. "How rude."

"I'm sorry." Henrik pressed his lips together, his expression serious. "It's just that we don't have many visitors like you. People will stare, I'm afraid. We've never had a telephone, either. I think most of our families would vote to settle on the moon before we put in a phone. They believe in roughing it, which means we do a lot of hard work and sweating. That's what is going to make this country great." He paused. "That and God's blessing."

"I see. Well, if you don't have a telephone, I'll need to hire a driver to take me out of here immediately."

Again Henrik wiped away a smile. "No drivers, Miss Emily. I'm afraid—"

"I'll thank you not to make a joke of this. My father is Major Alan Parkinson, and he'll be looking for me."

Henrik bowed at the waist. "Well, then, Major Parkinson's

daughter, I'll ask some of the kibbutz leaders what we can do for you. We don't want anyone thinking we kidnapped you, do we?"

"That is *exactly* what happened."

"A misunderstanding, I'm sure." Henrik smiled again. "Not surprising, though, with all the commotion last night."

"He wouldn't listen—"

"He never does." Henrik nodded and held up his hand. "But you heard what he said when he dropped you off. Most of the roads coming into Kibbutz Yad Shalom are blocked or very dangerous. I'm surprised you made it at all."

"Perhaps. But as that's the case, why isn't someone *doing* something about these roads instead of just throwing this silly party?" Emily spun around and waved at the festival of people.

"Oh, it's not a typical party," Henrik corrected her. "It's—"

"Hag Habikurim," Dov finished the sentence a little sourly.

"That's right." Henrik went on as he led them to one of the small barns. " 'Observe the feast of weeks with the first-fruits of the wheat harvest.' Isn't that what it says in Exodus?"

Another Torah scholar, Dov thought as he followed in Henrik's footsteps. *Like Uri on the* Aliyah.

The older boy stopped and turned. "By the way, I didn't catch *your* name?"

Dov didn't answer for a moment. This Henrik Melchior was too friendly.

"Or maybe it's top secret," Henrik laughed. "If it is, I can give you a good Danish name, if you like. Jørgen. Ib. Aage. You probably wouldn't be able to pronounce any of them anyway. Of course, nobody can, except the Danes."

Dov could see that the other boy was trying to make them feel welcome and better about being stuck in such a place. But it wouldn't work. Still, what would it hurt to give his name?

"Dov. My name is Dov…Zalinski."

"All right, then. That's a start. Dov…and Emily. No relation, I suppose. But there seems to be some connection between you two all the same, from what your traveling partners tell me. Now, Zalinski has to be a Polish name, am I right? And Dov is Hebrew."

At least Henrik pronounced his name right. *Dove*, as in "He *dove* into the ocean." Dov wondered what anyone had told Henrik about him, besides the fact that he and Emily had both been dumped into the truck last night at the same time.

"You're not very talkative, are you? That's all right." Henrik carried both ends of their conversation. "As I was saying, we're celebrating the Feast of the Firstfruits. It wouldn't be right not to celebrate, no matter *what* is happening outside."

Dov wondered just what was going on "outside," as Henrik put it, besides mobs throwing rocks at passing trucks.

"And things will get better as soon as Matthias arrives," Henrik told them. "You'll see. He's my stepfather, and he works for the Swedish Red Cross. But he comes to the kibbutz as often as he can—usually every few weeks."

"The Swedish Red Cross?" Emily looked as if she was making a connection.

Dov remembered the man who had visited the refugee ship, too. He fingered the unusual Star of David pendant in his pocket, an odd gift from the man.

"Tall man?" asked Emily. "Blond beard?"

Henrik nodded, and his face lit up.

"Black-rimmed spectacles?"

"You've met him, then?" asked Henrik. "Where? When?"

Emily looked at Dov as if expecting him to say something, but he just looked away. If she wanted to chat, *she* would have to do the explaining. Dov just hoped she would leave out the part about falling off the *Aliyah*, and how she saved his life by swimming with him to the beach.

"We met him back on the refugee ship that he…Dov came from. I went with my father to help translate, and your father was there, too."

"*Step*father," Henrik corrected her. "My real father…he, uh, died in Sweden."

"I'm sorry," replied Emily politely.

They followed Henrik away from the party, past a well-tended garden and up to a cluster of simple wooden sheds. Henrik acted as if he enjoyed playing the host, showing them around. He'd been at the kibbutz for only a few months, he said, but he liked working in the chicken house. The birds reminded him a little of the homing pigeons he and his friends Peter and Elise Andersen used to raise back home in Denmark.

"Oh, but I keep forgetting," he told them with a smile. "*This* is home now."

He turned to the shed door and twisted a four-number combination on a hefty-looking gray padlock.

Odd, thought Dov. *They must have some valuable chickens in there.*

"My stepfather, Matthias, knew the man who started all this," continued Henrik, flipping the door open. "Which is probably why Matthias, my mother, and I have been able to stay here on the kibbutz, even though we're kind of…different."

Different, how? Dov wondered but didn't ask. He would probably find out soon enough. Besides, Henrik looked ready enough to explain on his own. The older boy stooped down and then handed Emily a few eggs to carry.

"They were close friends until the old man died."

"I see." Emily nodded.

"His name was Cohen, but Matthias always called him the Peace Rebel. He was Matthias's teacher years ago."

"I thought you told us your stepfather was from Sweden," said Emily.

"Oh, he was." Henrik nodded. "But Matthias came here to Palestine to work and learn for a couple of years back in the twenties or thirties. They both wrote letters when Matthias returned home, too."

"What did you say he called this Mr. Cohen? A rebel?"

"The Peace Rebel." Henrik smiled. "Sort of like the Messiah was when He made friends with tax collectors and sinners. I guess old Mr. Cohen was the same way, always going against what people thought he should do, like a rebel. He also made friends with people he wasn't supposed to make friends with. The Arabs, I mean. So Matthias called him the Peace Rebel. Kind of an odd nickname, don't you think?"

Dov thought about the Arabs who had met them on the road last night and wondered what the old Peace Rebel would have done.

Henrik went on. "Matthias told me that Cohen wanted this farm to be a place where the settlers would make peace with the people around them. That's why he called it Kibbutz Yad Shalom."

"Monument to peace," put in Emily. She held on to her growing collection of eggs, trying not to crack them.

"You know some Hebrew! Good. You'll fit in around here. You could even help teach some of the new arrivals." Henrik smiled again, and Dov caught himself almost smiling along. He would have to watch out for this fellow and his smiles. It was almost like catching a yawn.

Emily looked away. "Yes, well...as I said, I must be contacting my father, Major—"

"You know, Miss Emily, I think if I were you I wouldn't tell anyone else that your father is in the British army. It won't make you very popular here on the kibbutz."

"Yes, well, of course." Emily wrinkled her forehead as she continued. "I just thought that perhaps ..."

As Henrik and Emily talked, Dov backed away slowly, turned a corner inside the small shed, and found an inside door secured by another large black padlock.

What's this? he wondered, pulling the door carefully. A beam of sunlight from a crack in the wall lit the room, but because of the lock he could pull the door open only enough to see the stacks of metal pipes inside.

Pipes? There were wooden boxes, besides, stacked floor to ceiling. He looked closer, pushing his nose through the crack in the side of the door.

No, not pipes. Dov wiped the dusty sweat from his brow and swallowed hard. *Enough rifles for an army!*

"Dov?" Henrik called his name.

Dov almost yelped with surprise, but caught himself and hurried back to where Henrik was collecting eggs, still telling his stories.

The older boy glanced at Dov when he stepped back around the corner. "So you noticed there are more than eggs in this building?"

Dov swallowed and wondered what to say. Was he supposed to know?

Henrik didn't wait for an answer, just handed him an egg. "Don't worry about it. You know, we should have brought a basket, but I wasn't thinking. Don't drop it, now."

The light from the main door suddenly dimmed as if a cloud had passed in front of the sun. Dov turned just in time to see the strong frame of a young man blocking his way out of the chicken house. In a heartbeat he knew who it was—the same person who had been staring at him when he was just waking up. The same one who had also been watching Emily.

"What are you doing here?" growled the man, and his voice seemed to rattle the walls. A chicken scurried away between his legs, but he paid it no mind. His face looked as if it had survived too many battles; his arms were as big around as Dov's legs. The man wasn't much taller than Dov, but with the threat in his pose, he seemed to tower over them.

"We're just leaving." Dov started for the door, but he might as well have tried to push through a brick wall.

Henrik and Emily stepped up from behind. "I was only showing them around the kibbutz, Moshe," Henrik explained. "They arrived last night with some others."

Dov planted his heels in the dirt floor, ready to drop his egg and put up his fists. It didn't matter how big this Moshe was.

Moshe studied him carefully, and a toothy smile broke across his face, unexpected like sun on a rainy day. "So! What a pair you make! And is this the girl who wants to go home to Daddy? A spy, perhaps?"

How much has he heard about Emily? Dov wondered.

"Come on, Moshe." Henrik tried to smile. "She's no more a spy than you are. They both just got off the *Aliyah* is what I hear. They jumped ship and swam to shore through British bullets."

Emily started to say something but must have changed her mind.

Dov was relieved. It probably was not the best time for her to tell her story.

"Really?" Moshe sounded interested. But just as quickly his expression turned sour, and he wagged a chunky finger in warning. "Yah, well...bullets or no bullets, you'd better keep an eye on these two, my Danish friend. And why don't you show them something nicer than this stinking chicken house, eh?"

Dov thought he saw the man's eyes glance in the direction of the gun room.

"Go on." Moshe backed up a step and waved his hand. "Get out of here."

Henrik pulled Dov with him through the door.

"Nothing in here besides a bunch of scrawny chickens." Moshe stared at Dov as they stepped out into the midmorning sunshine.

"That and a bunch of dusty old guns," Dov blurted out.

"What did you say?" Moshe hissed and moved toward him.

LAST-MINUTE WARNING

Dov refused to back away from Moshe's challenge. He wasn't going to stay at the kibbutz for long, not when he was going to find his family. What did guns hidden in a chicken coop mean to him?

"You heard what I said. There are guns in the chicken coop."

Henrik turned slowly to face him, a pained expression on his face.

"Tell him I don't know what guns he's talking about, Henrik." Moshe looked as if he would strangle the Danish boy. "We have no guns on this kibbutz, other than the one we're supposed to have. Right, Henrik?"

Henrik only shook his head, put up his hands, and shrugged in surrender.

"I don't care about your guns," Dov told Moshe. "I don't care about any of this."

"Yeah, well you'd better remember that if any *English* ever ask." Moshe looked long and hard at Emily. "We only have one. Any more would be illegal. Understand?"

Dov noticed that Emily looked very, very pale in the bright

sunlight.

"And don't listen to that stuff Henrik will tell you. Did he quote you that 'He who lives by the sword dies by the sword' rubbish?" Moshe was now only inches from Dov's face. "He's just like my father. Probably going to die just like my father did, too, because he won't fight."

And you'll fight, obviously. Dov didn't dare say it aloud.

"The Arabs will push us into the sea if we don't show them how strong we are. You want them to do that to us, now that you've made it to Eretz Israel? Whose side are you on?"

"*My* side," snapped Dov. It sounded like a clever thing to say, though he didn't quite know what he meant by it. "But I will tell you that I'm not going back into the ocean. I've already been there."

"Hmm." Moshe looked satisfied with Dov's answer. "All right, then. Maybe there's hope for you. But get out of here and leave the chickens to Henrik from now on. That's about all he's good for."

Moshe slammed the door shut, spun the lock combination, and mumbled something to Henrik about talking to him later before he strode away.

Henrik waited until the man was out of hearing to say anything. "You need to stay away from him," he finally told them. "He's trouble."

"Quite," echoed Emily.

"I suppose." Dov shrugged and turned away. He liked Henrik well enough. But he couldn't just trust him and his word. Not yet, anyway. And he certainly wouldn't let the boy tell him what to do.

"You don't understand." Henrik caught Dov's arm and spun him around.

"I understand enough. You're scared of him."

"No." Henrik shook his head. "I'm trying to help you."

"You don't even know me."

"Maybe not. But you don't know who Moshe Cohen is, either."

Dov didn't answer.

"Cohen." Emily wrinkled her nose, thinking. "Any connection to . . . ?"

"There are a lot of Cohens." Henrik nodded his head. "But the Moshe Cohen you just met is the founder's youngest son."

"The Peace Rebel? *His* son?" Emily's eyes were wide.

Henrik nodded. "Listen, it gets worse. This Moshe . . . we can't prove it, but some people think he's with the"—he lowered his voice—*"Irgun!"*

Henrik pronounced the word *ear-goon*, looking at them as if they should understand what it meant. He said it like someone might say *the enemy*, or *the plague*—or something worse.

"Do you know who the Irgun are?" he asked, but Dov didn't answer. "They're Jewish terrorists! They used to be part of the *Haganah*, the Jewish Defense Force, but not anymore. They're too rough, too violent. In fact, I've heard Moshe was part of the group that blew up the King David Hotel in Jerusalem last year."

Emily shuddered and turned away.

"Now he gives military training to some of the men here at the kibbutz, even though that's *not* what this place is all about. He thinks there's going to be a war with the Arabs, and . . ." His voice trailed off, as if he realized he'd said too much. "Do you understand?"

Dov understood. And by the look of it, so did Emily. Her face had turned even paler at Henrik's mention of the King David Hotel.

"I don't mean to scare you," said Henrik. "And maybe it's

all a rumor. Still …"

"I understand," she mumbled, leaning against the side of the chicken coop for support. "And I simply must get out of here. Now more than ever."

You and me both, thought Dov. He would find his parents before matters in Palestine grew worse. He had to.

"I'm sorry." Henrik's gentle smile returned. "Listen, you've had a rough welcome. But this is life in Eretz Israel. Just remember that I'm on your side."

What side are we on? Dov wondered as Henrik and Emily wandered back to the festival. As if it would help him think, he felt in his pocket for the Star of David Matthias had given him back on the *Aliyah*. The Star of David with the cross in the middle—a *Magen* David.

Whose side am *I really on?* he asked himself. Before today he hadn't even known there were so many. Moshe's rifle-toting side? Or Henrik's side, the side of the Peace Rebel?

✡ ✡ ✡

The next morning Emily made sure she wasn't the last to get up. As soon as she heard one of Henrik's roosters crowing, she shot out of the hard cot she had been given, straightened the single green wool blanket, and headed out the door of the crude sleeping cabin. She took a deep breath of morning air, with its pungent aroma of freshly mown hay on the hills. Three or four families were already at work in the cucumber patch, hoeing weeds.

For a moment she enjoyed the quiet of dawn, the smell of the fields, the sounds of people working.

Good morning, God. It was a good time to pray. Mornings were always the best for prayer, she thought. *That is, when I remember.*

Will the roads clear today? She wished God would answer her. *Please, God, just long enough for me to escape this dreadful place and get home to Jerusalem.*

She thought her situation sounded like something out of an adventure book, only this was real. What a horrible mess! And what about Daddy and Mum? What if they thought she were . . . ?

Oh dear! What else *could* her parents think after the disaster on the *Aliyah*? The thought hit her hard. *I must get home, or at least get them a message. They need to know I'm alive!*

"Good morning!" crowed Henrik nearly as loudly as his roosters.

Emily jumped as the older boy came up behind her at a trot. He had no right to sound so cheerful.

"I see you're not worried about running into Moshe this morning."

Moshe. In the far corner of the kibbutz, under the shadow of the guard tower, Moshe and his men were practicing with their pretend guns, broomsticks, like boys playing war.

"Moshe? Certainly not. I hadn't given him a thought." Emily ran a hand through her hair and wondered how awful it looked. How many days had it been since she'd washed it properly? What bugs had taken up residence there? Finding a bathtub was high on her list.

"Hmm." Henrik didn't sound as if he believed her put-on bravery as they walked toward the clucking and squawking of the hens.

Emily didn't mind the noisy birds, but the sound of a distant engine caused her to glance at the dusty road to the kibbutz. A dirty black car was barreling in at the head of a dust cloud. It sputtered to an abrupt stop in the gravel, just in front of the dining hall.

"What on earth is that?" Henrik quickly joined the others who streamed out of the dining hall.

Emily followed, and it was all she could do to keep from jumping up and down. *At last!* she wanted to yell. *My ride home!*

At the very least it could be her ride out of Kibbutz Yad Shalom. Emily had no idea how the car had made it through the dangerous roads past stone-throwing mobs or worse, but here it was. In the backseat, four unwashed, wide-eyed children pressed their noses to the side window, staring back at Emily and Henrik.

"Welcome, welcome." A tall, older woman with a quick step and short-cropped gray hair hurried up to the car and pulled open the back door. The four children drew back as if they had been attacked. Emily guessed not one was over ten years old.

"Got some more orphans for you," announced the driver, emerging from his side. He sounded as if he were delivering a package someone had to sign for. "Smuggled in crates from a refugee ship, is what I hear. My contacts in Haifa said you'd be able to care for them here at Yad Shalom."

Between his thick wad of gum and unusual accent, Emily had a hard time understanding the man.

The gray-haired woman looked around for help. "You there, young lady." She pointed straight at Emily. "You look as if you need something to do. Come give me a hand with these children."

Emily checked behind her to make sure the woman didn't mean someone else, but she knew an order when she heard it. Slowly she stepped forward.

"Hurry up, now!" insisted the woman. She reached in and fished out one of the children.

Emily tried to do the same.

"You're safe now," the woman told the fear-faced children, as if the words could instantly erase their fear. "Do you understand? *Farshtain? Comprendez? Hevin?*"

She tried in English, Yiddish, French, and Hebrew. Nothing got a response. Judging by the four wide-eyed expressions, the young refugees didn't understand a word the woman was saying.

Emily tried to take the smallest girl's hand, but she would have none of it.

"Ouch!" Emily jerked her hand back to see a red row of teeth marks on the soft part of her palm. "You bit me!"

"Here, why don't you let me help?" Henrik had come up quietly behind them.

Emily backed away gladly.

The children tried to hide from Henrik, too, but not for long. Emily watched as he reached behind the ear of the youngest in the bunch, the one who had bitten her on the hand.

"What's this?" he asked the little girl, pulling a small coin from behind her ear. She didn't know and was soon giggling shyly at Henrik's tricks. It wasn't five minutes before Henrik had turned from the car with two small children under his arms. One was holding up her tiny silver prize, grinning and sampling it with her ever busy teeth.

Henrik winked as he walked by. "You just have to know how to handle them," he told Emily with a smile. "Give them something besides your hand to chew on."

The last two children from the car followed on their own, though fear was still carved into their faces. They reminded Emily of the children on the *Aliyah*, the ship Dov had escaped from. They had seen too much.

But Emily didn't have time now to think about the *Aliyah*. She could hear shouts as a kibbutz girl sprinted toward them on the dirt road, from the direction of the main gate.

"Soldiers!" yelled the girl in a voice almost too breathy to understand. She was perhaps Henrik's age. Bursts of dust exploded under her bare feet as she closed the last hundred yards.

"Soldiers...coming!" The bronze-faced girl waved her arms to get their attention. The scarf on her head flew off, and her black hair tumbled around her shoulders and into her face. "British jeeps! Ariel tried to hold them off at the gate, but they're coming in from the highway, fast."

"All right," Henrik told the girl. "To the chicken coop. You help Ruben hide the new ones from the *Aliyah*. We'll take Dov and these four children to the well."

The other girl disappeared across the courtyard in the direction of the sheds. They must have practiced this before, Emily decided, as she waited for the soldiers to come. She, for one, was glad to think her time at the kibbutz was ending.

Henrik tightened his hold on his two orphans. "This way!" he urged them.

The older woman pulled the other two new arrivals, now more frightened than ever, by the hand.

"Dov!" Henrik motioned with his head. "Come with us. Hurry!"

INTO THE TOMB

6

Henrik was deadly serious, and Dov could guess why. No one expected a visit from British soldiers. And Dov, like most of the children at the kibbutz, didn't have the legal papers to be in the country. So if any soldiers were to ask...well, it would be better, Dov knew, if that didn't happen.

Without a word, Dov followed Henrik, an older woman he hadn't met yet, and four nervous-looking young children to a spot behind the dining hall. Henrik stopped in front of a square cement box with a wooden door about the size of a small kitchen table on top.

"What's this?" asked Dov, stopping with the others. He thought he could hear jeeps on the lane only a few hundred yards away, on the other side of the main building.

"It's our well. You're going to hide there with these children."

Dov pulled back. "If you think I'm—"

"Stop worrying!" Henrik was all business this time, no smiles. "We've planned for this, so you won't be in the water at all. There's a rope ladder for you to climb down and a board at the bottom to stand on. I'll hand you the children."

Dov took one look at the dark, damp hole and stopped. Two of the children whimpered, but they seemed to understand what was happening and how serious it was. Maybe they had done this kind of thing before.

"Dov, you can stand out here and let them take you away, or you can hide. It's your choice."

A jeep came to a brake-screeching halt and the decision was made. Dov gripped his hands together to keep from shaking as he swung his leg over the cement wall. He could smell the damp, dark air below him, like that of a cave.

Or a tomb.

"Hurry!" urged the woman. She handed Dov one of the children, a little boy about five years old, who was shaking, too.

"Hey!" Dov slipped on the second rung of the rope ladder and came face-to-face with the boy, who asked him something in his own language, pleading with him. Dov could only shake his head. "You'll be fine," Dov promised him, but now that they were down in the black hole he was not at all sure.

The oldest of the four children followed Dov down the swaying ladder. He couldn't have been more than seven years old. They went down five feet, ten feet, deeper, and then stopped on a wooden board about six feet long, hung like an extra-wide swing from two ropes. Dov looked up to the bright square of sunshine just as the door slammed shut with a crash.

"Oh!" Dov gasped before he could stop himself. The children clung to him like puppies to their mother. All they could do was look up and listen.

"It's going to be all right," Dov whispered to his brood, but he wasn't sure he believed it himself. "Just a little game of hide-and-seek, only nobody's going to find us. Now, sit down before we fall off this thing and drown."

No one answered, but the children held on to one another and sat down after Dov did, causing their perch to sway slightly. One whispered to the others in a language Dov didn't understand. Russian, maybe. Dov had heard Russian a few times before—enough to know what it sounded like.

After a few minutes in the well, Dov found it wasn't quite as dark as he'd first thought. Sunlight trickled through cracks in the warped wooden door above. Sounds, too, but only ghostly echoes of what was happening up in the world of light.

Dov didn't dare look down, so he had no idea how far above the water they dangled. He didn't want to know, either, but found out quickly enough when the girl to the left of him dipped her toe in the water with a little splash. It was just below where they sat.

Dov shivered. He felt as if he had died and been buried, and when their board began to tip, he steadied himself with an arm around the rope ladder. Again he found himself fingering the six-pointed Magen David in his pocket—as if it would somehow help him. The children huddled quietly on either side of him. How had he gotten himself into such a mess?

"Baruch Ata Adonai, Elohenu . . ." Dov's lips whispered the start of an ancient Hebrew prayer before he even realized what he was saying. Where had the prayer come from? It must have been something his father had once prayed, or maybe Rabbi Ben Salomon back in Czestochowa. But Dov could remember no more than the first line, which he kept repeating, quietly, so the kids wouldn't hear how scared he was. The door shut tightly above them was the only thing protecting them from the eyes of the soldiers. What if something gave them away? What would Dov do if the soldiers opened the door

and found them hiding like rats in the dark hole?

"Baruch Ata Adonai," he began again, his lips trembling. *"Elohenu Melech ha'olam ..."*

Blessed art Thou, O Lord, our God, King of the universe ...

Again, the words reminded him of the father he had almost forgotten. The one he had come to Eretz Israel to find, if he could.

But why was he saying this prayer? He couldn't remember ever praying before, not on his own. Well, maybe when he was a little boy, back when he'd lived with his imma and abba and big brother, Natan, on Gensia Street in Warsaw, where there were flower boxes on the windows and kids playing tag on the street. He might have prayed back then. Back then, it made sense to him.

Since the war, though, he'd forgotten how to pray. Or even whom to pray to. And after what he'd seen in the Nazi camps—well, he didn't ever want to think about that part of his life again.

Again the ancient prayer tumbled off his tongue.

To his surprise, after a couple of minutes the kids joined in. *"Shehech'eyanu,"* they said. Here was a language they all understood. *"V'kimanu v'higgi'yanu lazman ha'zeh."*

Deep inside he knew what the words meant, even after all the years that had passed since he'd learned it. So did the little ones holding on to him for dear life.

...who has kept us alive and preserved us to reach this time.

✡ ✡ ✡

Time seemed to fade in the dark. Had it been an hour? Two? Dov wasn't sure. At least he and the children were able to whisper to each other in old Hebrew prayers, like the *Shema.*

"Shema Israel Adonai Eloheinu Adonai echad."

Hear, O Israel, the Lord our God, the Lord is one.

And the Jewish prayer called the *Kaddish*, which began, *"Yisgadal v'yiskadash sh'may raba ..."*

Glorified and sanctified be God's great name ...

The two older children knew more of the words than the others; sometimes they knew more of the prayers than Dov. They whispered the words over and over. It kept the children from crying, and helped keep Dov's mind off what might be happening above them.

They couldn't ignore the sounds above them entirely, though. Especially not when they could hear men's voices just above them, echoing. What were they saying?

Finally Dov had to know. "Stay here," he whispered to the boy huddled next to him, hoping the tone of his voice would help the boy obey. Dov slowly, carefully tried the rope ladder. When he was at the top, he lifted the door with his head just enough to see Emily arguing with two British soldiers who had their backs to him. Where was Henrik?

"But you must believe me!" She wrung her hands and looked around as if someone were chasing her. "My father is—"

"Major Parkinson. Yes, so you say. Works at Command HQ, Eighty-seventh Airborne." A sergeant with three stripes on his upper arm stepped back toward the well. If Dov had wanted to, he could have reached out and yanked the officer by the pant legs.

"Yes, and—"

"I believe you, miss. Although, I certainly don't know what you're doing *here*."

"I tried to explain it to you, Sergeant. My father—"

"He's not my commander, you understand. But I *can* try to get word to him."

"You're saying you cannot give me a ride home?"

"I'm sorry. We have our orders to search this kibbutz farm for illegals, then return to base immediately. Not go to Jerusalem under any circumstances."

"Oooh!" Emily crossed her arms. "Just you wait until my father hears about this. He's—"

"It won't help to threaten us, young lady. As I said, we'll try to notify your parents and send someone to come pick you up."

That would have to be good enough for Emily. Dov thought he heard her sigh.

"By the way, miss, I'm terribly thirsty. Is this a well?" The British officer started to turn around.

"Um, yes, it's a well, but …" Emily fumbled for words.

Dov ducked his head and let down the lid of the well as quietly as he could. He held his breath, trying not to make a sound. Why had he risked the climb to the top?

"But, see here." Emily wasn't giving up. "I really don't see why you can't take me out of here."

"It's not that we wouldn't like to, miss," the sergeant said. "It's just against orders, you see, and right now it's not safe besides."

"Safe? What about my being safe here on this kibbutz? Can you guarantee that?"

"No. Certainly these Jews picked about the worst place for a settlement in all of Palestine. Arab villages all around. When those fellows attack, there won't be much His Majesty's army can do for you. We're being shot at out there, you understand. The roads are a war zone. It's certainly no place for a young lady such as yourself."

"That's what I've been trying to *tell* you." Emily sighed. "But if you won't take *me*, you'll have to at least take a note to my father. He doesn't even know I'm alive."

The sergeant was quiet for a moment. "All right, give me your note, and I'll see what I can do. Now, about that drink. I suppose the water's clean?"

"I'll get it for you," replied Emily. There was no time for Dov to get down the ladder before the top creaked open and sunlight flooded his dungeon. The Russian children below gasped at the light, and Emily stared at Dov's face in wide-eyed surprise. She had to have known he was there, of course, but still it must have startled her to see he was so close.

"Oh!" Emily flinched, then recovered.

Dov gripped the rope ladder and tried not to slip any farther while Emily lowered her bucket down on a rope to get a drink for the Englishman. "I'll have it for you in just a moment."

"Splendid."

Dov stood still and tried not to get in the way of the bucket. A minute later Emily closed the lid, and not long after that Dov heard the sergeant shouting at his men. But no more Emily; she must have given him her note and left.

"We're wasting our time here, Sergeant Wicks," said one of the other soldiers. "Don't you think, sir?"

"Sure enough," the sergeant replied. "Let's just be gone before the Arabs attack this 'orrid place. There's going to be lettuce soup and a chicken potpie waiting for us back at base, and I, for one, am getting hungry."

"And the girl's note, sir? When should we deliver it?"

"Oh, *that*?" The sergeant chuckled. "You think I have time to play postman? She's likely an impostor anyway. They're very clever, you know."

The door above Dov's head squeaked open just a crack, and Dov looked up in time to feel a wadded-up piece of paper hit him square in the face.

Emily's note.

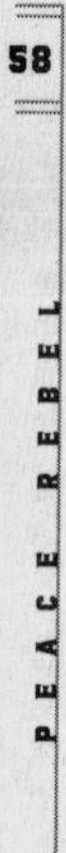

THE ILLEGAL

Emily watched as the dust settled behind the British army jeeps leaving the kibbutz and tried her best not to cry. Why wouldn't they take her away from here? At least they had the note to her father. Perhaps that was the answer to her prayer, she thought. Daddy would come to get her right away.

"Dust get in your eyes?"

That annoying Henrik again! Emily turned away and dabbed the corner of her eyes with her sleeve. She certainly didn't want to cry in front of anyone.

"Yes, as a matter of fact," she snapped back. "That's all you seem to have here in abundance."

"Oh, I don't know. It's different than Denmark, but I like it just the same."

"I'm glad for you," she said, though she wasn't. She watched as Henrik helped Dov and the others out of their hiding place.

"You should be grateful I didn't betray you to the soldiers," she told Dov. Perhaps she *should* have.

"What?" Dov got to his feet and stared at her.

"You are an illegal immigrant, after all. And when I get back home, I'm going to tell my father about your coming into the country against the law."

Emily crossed her arms, as if to settle the issue. That's what Daddy would have done. It always seemed to work for him. Why didn't anything ever work for her?

"You tell him whatever you like." Dov shrugged. "I don't care."

The nerve of this cheeky boy, after all she'd done for him! If only she had stayed closer to her father back on the immigrant ship. Or better yet, if only she had stayed with her mother and went to Tel Aviv rather than become caught up in this whole messy affair at this horrid kibbutz.

"Well, my father will come for me," she finally told him. "You'll see."

"No, he won't." Dov looked too smug, as if he knew a secret she didn't.

Emily gritted her teeth together and felt every muscle in her body tighten. If only she were a boy, she would show him! Perhaps she would anyway.

"He will, too!" she almost shouted. "The soldiers promised!"

This time Henrik had to jump into the middle of their battle.

Dov frowned, backed up a step, and fished a soggy piece of paper out of his pocket. He threw it into the dust at her feet. "See for yourself."

That smug look again. Emily narrowed her eyes and threw daggers at him with her stare.

Henrik stretched out his arms to keep Emily and Dov away from each other and picked up the paper. "It's a note of some kind, Emily."

"I know perfectly well what it is!" She recognized the writing, recognized the piece of paper. Before they could see her cry again, she spun away and ran.

✡ ✡ ✡

Emily was glad no one tried to follow her. But she didn't get far before she ran into the group of Russian orphans. Emily couldn't help it; she stopped and watched them as they played. As she did, she felt the anger slip away.

How could I have said such stupid things?

She hoped she wouldn't have to see Dov or Henrik anytime soon. Henrik reminded her of Aunt Rachel, the way he talked about the Messiah. And Dov, well, he was just annoying sometimes.

Emily kept to a shadow, and the orphans ignored her for the moment. That was fine. They seemed so intense for children, not laughing, not smiling. This game of theirs was serious business.

They lined up, and, holding on to each other, made a chain. Emily didn't understand their words, but she recognized the game—nearly the same as one she had once played back in England. The boy on the end of the queue kicked an empty tin as they whipped around in a circle, and the rest of them ran to find hiding places as it clattered across the dirt.

The can rolled to a stop at Emily's feet. She turned to kick it back but was surprised to look down into the dark green eyes of a young girl—the same one who had bitten her hand.

"Oh!" Emily began, and she backed away.

But the little girl wasn't upset. She tugged at Emily's sleeve as if to say, "Help me hide."

"Well …" This time Emily stumbled after her new little friend while looking around to make sure no one else saw her playing. It wouldn't do to have them see her—wouldn't be proper, her being the major's daughter and their being illegal refugees. But...perhaps just this once.

Emily followed her friend to a hiding place behind a farm wagon. The girl squatted quietly and watched for their chance. A moment later it was time to run back to the can, as fast as they could. The girl screamed as they neared the safety of home base, and at first Emily didn't notice Dov standing there, watching the children playing.

She skidded to a stop and peeled away her new friend's hand.

"Are you going to turn these illegals in, too?" he asked.

Emily looked away.

"You turn *me* in," Dov continued, "and you turn in all of these kids."

"I don't want to discuss it with you." Emily had had enough of this argument; clearly Dov wasn't going to let her apologize for her earlier words. She felt her cheeks redden. "You're just a...a twit. A complete and utter *twit*!"

The name didn't seem to affect the Jewish boy. Probably he'd been called worse things.

"I don't care what you call me. I don't need your help anymore."

"You needn't fret about that." Emily rolled her eyes. "Did I say I was going to help you?"

"Well, let me tell you something." He pointed east, toward the low hills. "When I find my family in Jerusalem, I'm not going to be an illegal, because *my* father, Mordecai Zalinski, he—"

"Oh, come, now," Emily interrupted. "You don't really think you're going to find your family here, do you? You came from the camps, right? When are you going to realize they're dead? *Gone.*"

The words echoed across the dusty courtyard, and Emily would have snatched them back if she could. Even if Dov *was* a twit, she couldn't take that hurt look on his face, as if she had slapped him.

Dov swallowed hard. His voice was low and hoarse. "You're wrong. I don't need you or anyone else to help me prove it, either. I'm going to find them *myself*!"

He shuffled off with his head down, raising a cloud of dust. Emily stared in silence, horrified at the cutting edge of her words. She couldn't remember being so angry with anyone in her life, but the anger drained away as quickly as air from a balloon. For once, she hoped, desperately hoped, she was wrong.

Her new friend tugged on her hand, but Emily shook her head no.

"Not this time," Emily whispered as she closed her eyes and turned away. All she wanted was to disappear.

Day three at Kibbutz Yad Shalom. Dov had told himself the night before that he wouldn't sleep late, that he wouldn't let anyone else wake before him. Maybe he would get up early enough to test the boundaries of the kibbutz, to see how well guarded they *really* were.

It didn't work.

"Dov?" The voice sounded like Henrik's, but Dov wasn't sure. He kept his eyes closed and rolled over on his cot so that his back was to the person who had dared disturb him.

"Dov, wake up." This time the hand on his shoulder told him it was no dream. Still, Dov couldn't quite shake the sleep that held him to the cot like a magnet. He groaned and opened one eye.

Only a thin sliver of pale yellow light framed Henrik in the opening of Dov's army-issue pup tent. The older boy squatted in the opening, looking intently at…

"Say, where did you get this?" Henrik picked up Dov's Magen David and held it to the light.

"That's mine!" Dov grabbed at the thief to protect his only treasure. He accidentally hit Henrik on the side of the head in his clumsy effort, hurting his own knuckle in the process.

"Ow!" Henrik staggered back. He dropped the star and held his head. "I was just looking."

"Oh." Dov scooped his treasure out of the dirt. "Well, I didn't mean to … I wasn't awake yet."

"That's okay." Henrik rubbed his head but grinned in the dim light. "That's what I get for trying to wake up a dead man."

"I'm alive."

"Good. You ought to be. It's past five o'clock, after all, and I'm going to need your help today in the fields."

"Ohh…" Dov groaned and rolled over. "Is *that* why you woke me?"

"The work will be good for you. Maybe it will help you take your mind off things. So put on a shirt and come with me. I'll show you what to do."

"No." Dov shook his head. "I've already worked enough… in Czestochowa. I'm done working."

Henrik scratched his chin for a moment and lowered himself back down to Dov's level.

"You don't understand, do you? Around here, all of us work, since all of us eat. You work, you eat. You don't work, you don't eat. Now, you want to eat, don't you?"

Dov thought it over for a minute. He felt a hard, bitter quivering in the pit of his stomach, as if he would either be sick or burst out crying at any second. But he kept it down, warning himself to grow up. He slipped on his shirt and followed Henrik down the path to the new fields.

"By the way, I hate to ask—" Henrik looked sideways with a smudge of a grin as they walked to the field—"since you might hit me in the side of the head again. But where did you get that Magen David?"

Dov walked a little farther, thinking. He might as well tell him.

"I got it from Matthias," Dov finally admitted. "Your stepfather."

Henrik stopped in his tracks. "No. Really? From Matthias?"

"It sort of...fell off the chain around his neck, and I picked it up. I didn't take it. He said I could keep it."

"I didn't say you took it. But could I see it again?"

Dov wasn't so sure.

"I won't take it from you," Henrik told him. "I promise."

Dov decided he would hold the pendant in his hand, not let the older boy touch it. He fished it from his pocket.

"I thought it looked familiar." Henrik smiled. "Do you know what it means, Dov?"

"What it means? It's just jewelry." Dov slipped it back into his pocket as they walked to the fields.

"Yes, but it still has meaning."

"It's just a Star of David."

"With a cross in the middle. The sign of Yeshua, the Messiah, inside the sign of David. You've heard about the Messiah, right?"

Dov wanted to plug his ears. Did he have to hear about "the Messiah" again? What good had this Messiah ever been to him?

"Rabbi Ben Salomon never talked about anyone named

Yeshua," Dov said, as if that would keep Henrik quiet.

"Was he your family's rabbi?"

"No, he was with me...at Czestochowa."

As soon as he'd said it, Dov wished he hadn't. He was talking too much.

Henrik nodded as though he was used to hearing people tell him their life histories.

"I've read about a rabbi who used to talk about the Messiah," Henrik went on. "You ever heard of the Thirteen Principles of Faith?" Henrik sounded as if he were teaching a *bar mitzvah* class, memorizing the Scriptures every Jewish boy learned to become a man.

Dov had to shake his head no. They had almost reached the field, a large, rocky hillside ringed by green grassy stubble and surrounded on the far side by a serious-looking barbed-wire fence.

"Well, one of them talks about waiting for the Messiah. I say He already came."

Came and went, maybe, Dov thought. *He's certainly not here now.*

"Maybe you don't believe that, but Matthias does, and so do I. That's what your Magen David means—the star with the cross inside."

"Oh." Dov didn't know what to think; he was almost glad they had reached the field.

Henrik led him to where they would be working behind a horse-drawn wagon.

"I said it before, but it's a good thing Matthias was friends with the founder, or I think they might have kicked us out of the kibbutz a long time ago." Henrik grinned and lowered his voice. "Jews who believe in the Messiah don't always fit in very well. But God has us here for a reason. You too, Dov."

Dov stared at the barren field. Had he come to Palestine

only to tug rocks out of this stubborn, sandy soil? This rock hauling was too much like the work camp, and Dov stayed away from anything that reminded him of the painful time. But here…he just couldn't shut out the memories.

And he couldn't keep the nervous, panicked feeling from rising in the pit of his stomach.

BATTLING THE MEMORY

8

"I can tell you're eager to get started." Henrik looked almost happy about working in the field of stones. He hoisted boulders as if they were nothing and began throwing them into the back of a waiting farm wagon. "See what we're doing? This is the first harvest."

"Of rocks?"

"Of rocks, yes, but it's still a harvest."

Dov wasn't so sure. Still, he tried to copy Henrik but either missed the back of the wagon or couldn't even lift the boulders.

"Oomph!" Dov grunted, bent his legs, and tried again.

Henrik looked at him and laughed. "Looks as if you'll need some help there, little bear!"

Little bear? Dov kicked at the rock and turned away. *Little bear.* Of course that's what his name meant, in Hebrew. But he didn't remember anyone ever calling him that, except his mother. Even so, he let Henrik help him the next time, and another fellow who was picking rocks with them. The three of them worked together while a fourth man drove the wagon slowly across the fields.

Dov didn't know how he had been talked into this. Even though it was early morning, the sweat dripped over his eyebrows, and he wiped his eyes with his sleeve to keep them from stinging. One stone only showed the way to another; it seemed there were more rocks than soil.

But Henrik—he sang, laughed with the men, told silly jokes about talking cows and homing pigeons, and patted Dov on the back once in a while. Once, when Dov forgot to be careful, he let himself be taken up in the rhythm of their work, even humming along with one of Henrik's silly songs before he caught himself.

Henrik winked at him. "Do you miss Poland, Dov?"

Miss it? No. He missed his family and his home, but too many years in Poland had been hard.

"I miss Denmark." Maybe Henrik didn't care if Dov answered or not. He heaved another rock into the truck. "I miss riding bikes with my friend Peter and going to his cousin's farm on the west coast. They had sheep there, and a nice place to swim. I especially miss my father, though. He died right after the war."

Dov just listened. He wasn't going to let the Danish boy trick him into talking about the things he missed.

"Do you miss your friends?"

Dov wondered what it would be like to have friends. He couldn't remember ever having one. He didn't know how to ride a bike, either, the way Henrik did. He shook his head.

"Not that I mind making new friends," continued Henrik. "You learn that, here in Israel."

Dov picked up a smaller rock and tossed it into the back of the wagon. He couldn't answer. A part of him wished he knew how to make friends as easily as Henrik, and he hid that part down deep.

When they'd piled up enough rocks to begin to make the wagon wheels sink, the driver took their load to the edge of the field and dumped the rocks into a larger pile. Other workers then took the rocks and wrestled them into a low, rambling fence. A couple of cows nibbled dried grass as they watched their progress.

"Where's Emily?" Henrik asked the fence builders. "I thought everyone was going to help today."

The men shrugged and shook their heads. None of them had seen Emily. In fact, nobody had seen her since the night before, not even the girls who were staying in her cabin.

Dov didn't worry himself about it, but he did wonder. *What is she up to?*

As the sun climbed in the sky, Henrik and the others stopped more often for drinks of water from a wooden bucket and breaks in the spot of shade under the wagon. But not Dov. He stood off to the side, his back to them, and tried to keep the unwanted memories pushed down.

But he couldn't, no matter how hard he tried. If he kept his eyes open, they stung from the sweat. That was better than closing them and seeing the nightmarish images from the munitions plant in Czestochowa, where he had watched overworked, starving, tortured Jewish slave laborers stumbling, falling, not getting up. Any sign of weakness was a death sentence.

"No!" Dov jumped when he felt hands on his shoulders from behind, but it was only Henrik.

"Whoa! I didn't mean to scare you. It's time for lunch."

Henrik looked at Dov as a doctor might look at a sick patient. "You need a break. Here, have a pita."

Dov had to admit he was ready to find out what the kibbutz women had brought out for them to eat. He bit into the flat, toasted pita bread sandwich stuffed with sliced cucumbers from the kibbutz garden, served with cups of cool, fresh raw milk that tasted almost like sweet cream. Dov gulped it all down greedily while still standing up. He'd honestly never tasted better.

"Relax. Sit down and eat," Henrik commanded him. All the other rock pickers and fence builders had already found shade behind the wagon.

Dov wiped the cream mustache from his lip, grabbed another piece of pita, and headed for a spot by the fence.

Henrik watched him leave. "You sure you don't want—"

"No."

Anywhere was better than sitting with everyone else, having to act pleasant, trying to pretend everything was all right. He dropped down at a spot next to a low bush on the edge of the field's barbed-wire border.

Nothing was right. Dov's arms ached from picking up and heaving rocks, and the sun beat heavily on his head. And everywhere, everything kept reminding him of the Nazi camps. Like ghosts, the memories crowded in on him until he hurt.

Dov shuddered and chewed, waving off a fly. One of the cows came over to investigate, and Dov backed up to keep out of the big animal's way. The barbed-wire fence behind him caught his shirt just below the shoulder.

He tugged, but that was the worst thing he could have done. Dov heard a tear as the sharp barb ripped away a patch in the back of his shirt, then felt the jagged claw dig into his skin and rake across his shoulder blade. He cried out in pain and terror at the suddenly too-real memory of a guard with tall black boots standing next to a fence just like this, ordering him to work harder, harder, harder.

Run! In his rising panic, Dov twisted the wrong way—straight *into* the fence. Anger took the place of fear, and the battle with the German guard, this place, this fence, began.

"No!" he cried. "No, no, no!" He fought this metal snake that grabbed at him and held him prisoner, pulling it, kicking it—anything to beat it to the ground. Barbs cut into his hands and arms, but Dov didn't care. He ripped and pulled, tugged and heaved, fighting this monster with more strength than he knew he had.

"Dov, what are you doing?" Someone tried to hold him back, but Dov pushed him away. He stomped and kicked until finally the barbed-wire fence lay quivering in the dust at his feet.

Dov fell to his knees as the tears came, this time with new strength. He had not cried like this since his mother had left him at the Warsaw orphanage when he was only five. Crying with tears he'd been storing up for a lifetime. He felt as if he had woken from a nightmare.

He buried his face in Henrik's shoulder without thinking. Embarassed, he tried to pull away, and his chest still heaved as he caught his breath. His arms were scratched and bleeding.

"Stop!" The wagon driver leaving the rock field waved desperately at them, pointing at something. What was the fellow so worked up about?

"The cow!" The driver pointed past them.

Dov turned just in time to see that one of the kibbutz's skinny chocolate-brown milk cows had wandered out through the break Dov had torn in the fence. In fact, the cow was yards away and kicking up dust in its search for greener pastures.

"I'll get it." Dov wiped his nose across the back of his hand and sniffled. "I let it out. I'll get it back."

"No, you won't!" Henrik grabbed Dov's arm. "We've been shot at in that field. No one is allowed out there, past the—"

Henrik didn't have a chance to finish his sentence. They heard two *pops* in the distance, then three. Then the stomach-churning sound of the cow bellowing in distant pain.

"They shot our cow!" yelled the wagon driver as he ran up to where they stood at the break in the fence line. "Our *best* cow."

"Ohh." Henrik turned away from the scene, and the pained look on his face made Dov feel worse than he already did. "Let's get this fence back up so that we don't lose any more animals."

The driver broke into a hurt-filled stream of bitterness in his old language. Romanian, maybe, or Albanian.

Dov didn't need to understand it to know it was his fault the cow had been shot. He left the field with his head down.

"I'm sorry," he muttered, not loudly enough for anyone to hear. "I can't help you. I'm no help to anyone. I've got to leave."

BETRAYED!

Now, this *is better!* Emily threw her head back and almost laughed as the wind whipped her hair. Dangerous it might be, but the safest way through these dangerous roads was in the backseat of a British army jeep. No one—Arab or Jew—would dare attack a British patrol like this, she thought.

At least I hope not.

They'd slipped out of Kibbutz Yad Shalom that morning much faster than she'd thought possible. "You're the major's daughter?" one soldier had asked her. It was as if he had seen Emily's note for help after all! She didn't recognize the man as one who worked for her father. He must have been new, just assigned to the Eighty-seventh Airborne Regiment in Jerusalem.

Not to worry. She'd always known her father would come for her, or at least send someone. Emily just wasn't certain how he'd managed. The soldiers who had searched the kibbutz yesterday must have passed on the word.

Of course, she hadn't stopped to say good-bye to anyone—there wasn't time. The kibbutz guard at the gate had let them through without a fuss. Now she smiled from ear to ear, thinking of what Daddy and Mum would say when they saw her again. Oh, but she looked a sight with her stringy hair and homemade kibbutz skirt. She would have to explain to Mum how her proper clothes had been ruined after she fell off the *Aliyah*. The first thing she'd do after she gave her parents hugs would be to have Ginger draw her a heavenly, steamy hot bath with a few drops of lavender water added—the Harris & Co. lavender water Daddy had brought her from London. She couldn't imagine anything more grand.

And what about Dov? She couldn't help feeling a sharp stab of guilt for the awful way she'd treated the Jewish boy, but it was too late to take back the mean words she'd spoken. Emily looked back over her shoulder through the choking dust, wishing she could have had a minute to say she was sorry. Just a minute.

Perhaps it's not all my fault, she told herself, trying to believe what she knew was not true. *I did what I could. I saved his life, for goodness' sake! And he was rude to me, too.*

Knowing that didn't make her feel any better, and she wondered what Dov would do now. Of course he wanted to find his family; she thought she understood a little of how desperate he must feel. And how alone. He would probably sneak around the country, asking for Mordecai Zalinski, and risk getting caught as an illegal immigrant. What if she didn't say anything to her father about Dov and let it go at that? Perhaps it would be best for everyone if she simply forgot she had ever met Dov.

Emily let the idea settle in her mind and held on to the sides of the backseat as the jeep screeched around a corner. She hadn't exactly been paying attention to their route, but the countryside didn't look familiar. It must be a shortcut on the way to the main highway to Jerusalem.

Or was it?

"I say, are we taking the long way home?" She tapped the driver's shoulder, but he didn't take his eyes from the road. He was dressed in the familiar khaki British soldier's uniform, crisscrossed by ammunition belts across his chest and topped by a jaunty beret. The man beside him held a large rifle at the ready as he scanned the roadside like a big-game hunter on safari. Neither one seemed inclined to talk.

"Hullo?" Emily decided to try again. "We're going rather fast!" She looked up at a rusty roadside sign, which told her what she had feared. They were *not* heading into the golden hills toward Jerusalem in the east, but straight along the coast—south.

"Tell her to get down," the driver mumbled to his partner through clenched teeth. "I see another car coming our way."

It wasn't what he said that suddenly sent a chill down Emily's spine. It was the language he spoke.

Hebrew.

A dozen "what if's" raced through Emily's confused mind, none of them good. British soldiers would surely not speak Hebrew to each other. These two men were not who Emily had thought they were!

The second man hesitated a second, and the driver barked his order once more. He was obviously in charge.

"Get down!" the second soldier finally ordered, turning to face Emily with a serious glare. Emily understood in a flash why he had not said anything; she could have kicked herself for not seeing it earlier. Soldier number two spoke in a high voice with a thick Hebrew accent, and her hair was stuffed up under her beret. There was no mistaking the threat on the woman's face.

"Now! Down!"

Emily could do nothing but obey. She ducked just as their jeep wandered into the oncoming lane enough to force another car to swerve and sound its horn. Their own driver nearly panicked, overcorrected, and hit the gravel shoulder before wrestling the jeep back into the right lane.

"Levi!" yelped the woman. The other car had whizzed by, going north even as they continued south. Emily saw enough to notice it was not another army jeep but an old American station wagon full of people, some waving out the windows like tourists. Surely they couldn't be on holiday in Palestine just now, could they?

The driver shook his head and glared at his partner. "Just keep her under control, Rivkah, will you?"

Emily thought of making a scene, but it was too late.

The driver unclipped the leather pistol holder on his belt to make sure Emily knew what could happen if she didn't follow orders.

"But, Levi—"

"Listen, Rivkah," he barked, never taking his eyes off the road, "you volunteered for this duty. It's too late for second thoughts."

"But she's just a *child*," answered Rivkah. "You didn't tell me she would be so young."

They obviously didn't know that Emily understood every Hebrew word they spoke.

"Did you expect a grandmother?" snapped the man. "Moshe said it was the major's daughter."

Moshe? Emily's ears pricked up at the name. There were a lot of Moshes in Palestine, she knew, but the hard-faced Moshe at the kibbutz came to mind. Could he have told these two about her arriving at Yad Shalom? How else would they have known?

"I should have asked for someone else to do this job with me." Levi was still obviously unhappy. "You're not—"

"I'll do the assignment." The woman pressed her lips together. "I didn't fail you at the King David, did I? And I told Moshe I would do this job. I'll keep my word. You don't need to worry."

Emily peeked at her kidnapper, who didn't strike Emily as someone likely to stay at the posh, expensive King David Hotel in Jerusalem. Oh, Rivkah was pretty, though not stylish in her army khaki. Her olive-toned skin and her smooth Hebrew told Emily she had been in Palestine awhile.

Still, the woman's disguise was good, very good. Every button was in place. No one seeing them speeding by in the jeep would have suspected they weren't looking at two British soldiers. They had made it this far, after all, past the station wagon full of daft tourists, past Arab villages, and, Emily supposed, even past other British.

"Where are you taking me?" asked Emily. The signs she saw told her they were speeding toward the little coastal city of Ashkelon.

"No questions," Rivkah told Emily in Hebrew. "I don't want to hurt you." But the pointed pistol she waved sent quite another message. Emily wondered if the gun shook from the bumpy road or because the woman was nervous. And now the woman didn't try to speak in English as the driver had back in the kibbutz. His English had been so proper and precise, in fact, that Emily hadn't given it a second thought. Until now.

"Now, you will stay perfectly still until I say you can get up," Rivkah advised Emily in a low, steady voice. There was no mistaking the steely edge to each word. "And you will do exactly as we say. Do you understand what I'm telling you?"

"I understand you," Emily answered in Hebrew before she

could realize her mistake. She buried her face in her hands, telling herself that she should not have answered that way. She should have pretended she only spoke English, and now it was too late.

"You speak Hebrew, eh? Good." The woman sounded pleased. "My English is not so good."

"What do you want with me?" Emily asked without looking up. To know that she was in such a mess made her ill. "My father will find you, and—"

"Don't threaten me. Be quiet and stay down."

They screeched around another corner on two wheels. Emily was afraid to even peek through her fingers, but she could not help hearing the normal sounds of honking horns, street vendors, and children playing. Finally they slowed a little.

"Don't even *think* about trying to run," Rivkah advised. "Look only at the ground, and get up when I say. Move only where I tell you. Or else."

Or else what? Emily didn't have to ask.

Their jeep turned a final corner and stopped in a splash of gravel.

"I'd feel a lot better if it were dark," growled Levi. "Get the door, Rivkah."

Emily heard the hinges of a shed door, squeaking and complaining. The jeep pulled ahead, and the door was bolted behind them. Emily squinted in the darkness.

"Eyes down!" Rivkah reminded Emily. "Out of the jeep."

Again Emily did exactly as she was told. There was still the matter of the gun, after all, and Emily had no doubt Rivkah knew how to use hers. Something slimy under her shoes told Emily that rubbish had probably been spilled all over the dirt floor. The place smelled of rotting melon rinds.

"Now follow me."

Emily did as she was told, following Rivkah out the door and back out into the sunshine. She kept her eyes glued down to the scruffy dirt street, which was littered with weeds, broken glass, and wrappers for Gilboa cigarettes.

Just like that, Emily was hurried inside the back door of a run-down house. Everything was dark and quiet, and it smelled musty and smoky, as if it had been closed up for months. The door slammed behind them, and Emily heard both a bolt and a chain.

"Sit down in that chair!" barked Levi.

"I can handle her," Rivkah objected, pulling out a chair. "She's not going anywhere."

"Just making sure."

"I *said* I can handle her, Levi."

The man grunted before he disappeared down a dim hallway. "See that you do."

THE AMERICANS INVADE

10

Dov was sure he could escape. Once out of Henrik's sight, he slipped behind a row of tents, then around the back of the dining hall, and aimed for the main road into Kibbutz Yad Shalom. For a moment he thought of trying to take something with him from the kitchen but decided against it. Someone would see him.

As for the Arabs beyond the kibbutz, they could do with him the same they had done to the cow, for all Dov cared. He just had to leave—and now.

He crouched behind the corner of the kitchen, waiting for two women to pass by. On their way to dinner duty, probably. He stepped out only to find himself in the path of a boxy, wood-paneled Ford Model A station wagon bumping down the main road, not ten yards from him.

Ah-OOO-gah! The driver sounded his horn and waved out the window through a cloud of dust.

Dov could only dive to the side as the ancient car sputtered to a stop in the kibbutz square. Steam puffed from the radiator, and the four doors squeaked open.

"Hey there!" cried a young man's voice. College age, and definitely American. "Are you all right, kid?"

Dov looked up to see a gorilla-sized boy—well, a man, really—staring down at him. He wore a short buzz cut and a *Yale University* sweat shirt. He held out his hand to help Dov to his feet, but Dov got up on his own power.

"You...speak...English?" asked the American loudly enough for anyone in the entire kibbutz to hear.

"A little," replied Dov. He would have escaped down the road, but by that time everyone else from the car had huddled around him. The driver and three other men almost as large. All dressed just as oddly, too, as if they had just come from some kind of outlandish American sports contest.

"I think we scared him, Stan," said a man in plaid trousers and a sweat shirt like Stan's, though with his thick glasses, he looked more suited to a quiet game of chess.

Stan nodded. "Yeah, my driving can be on the wild side, but it's necessary in these parts. Why, this morning we nearly had a head-on with a couple of crazy Brits in a jeep, down the road a piece." Stan motioned up the road. "And now you. You sure you're okay? You scratched your arms up pretty badly."

The man in plaid didn't wait for Dov's answer. "We'da been road kill between here and Haifa ten times over if it weren't for Stan. He's the best driver there is!"

The others in the traveling troop clapped for their leader and nodded their "amens."

"Say, this place is the real thing, isn't it?" Stan asked. "The tour brochure said so. So far we've floated like corks in the Dead Sea and stood where Elijah beat up the prophets of Baal on Mount Carmel. Now it's time to live on a genuine koo-boots, or whatever you call it."

Dov nodded, afraid to say anything, as Stan continued. The

American put out his hand again and grinned to show his shiny collection of pearly white teeth. "By the way, I'm Stan Loftin, and we call ourselves the N-P-Y-A-C-C-H-'47-G-T. We made arrangements several months ago to visit a real key-bootsk while we're traveling around Palestine. Thought it would be a swell place to see."

Dov stared at him blankly. Stan had said he spoke English, but maybe American English wasn't as close to England's English as Dov had always thought it was.

"The name stands for the North Philadelphia Young All-Church Council Holyland '47 Goodwill Tour," Stan continued, taking Dov's limp hand and pumping it like a well handle. "That's Chip's idea for a name. We're from Pennsylvania, USA, and we've come to share the love of the Lord with you all."

Dov nodded blankly, thinking this was what it might be like to meet a stranger from another planet. The chess player in plaid pulling bags out of the open back end of the Ford was named Chip Clevenger. The other two were Les and Clarence, Stan and Chip's younger friends and freshmen at Temple University.

"We heard there was a little trouble, but it's more like a near war," explained Stan. "We figure we'll be all right, though. We're protected, if you know what I mean." He grinned and pointed his thumb toward the clouds. "But, man, you ought to put some bandages on those scrapes, kid."

"Oh, *there* you are!" Henrik's voice carried across the dusty kibbutz courtyard. He led a ragged troop of rock pickers back from the field. "I wasn't sure you four would make it. We hadn't heard—"

"You must be Henry!" boomed Stan. He turned to smile even more broadly at Henrik. "So you *did* get our letter. I was afraid it hadn't gotten through. Mind if I call you Hank?"

"Uh …"

Dov took the chance to slip out of the crowd, away from the greetings and handshakes, away from the comments on his scratches and cuts. Now that the fieldworkers had returned, it had to be past dinnertime. His noisy stomach convinced him to stay for dinner after all.

Without wanting to, he found himself looking in the crowd for Emily. Maybe she had been talked into working in a far field, the way he had been.

Maybe.

Rivkah tossed a newspaper onto the table in front of Emily, front page up.

"You read Hebrew as well as you speak it?" asked the woman. It didn't sound exactly like a compliment, but Emily supposed she could have said worse.

She looked down at the paper, startled by the fuzzy photo of a rusty old freighter leaning far to the side, barely afloat. She instantly recognized it as the same ship she had been on with her father only a few days ago.

Ten Missing in Aliyah *Incident, Presumed Drowned* read a large headline below the photo. Then below that in smaller letters: *Daughter of British Major Also Drowns, Body Not Yet Recovered.*

They're talking about me*! They think* I … Emily shuddered at the thought and how her parents must be hurting. *If only they knew the truth!*

"Looks like you're famous," drawled the woman. She sucked at an ugly stub of a cigarette and filled the room with bitter blue smoke. "And maybe not as dead as everyone thinks."

When Rivkah wasn't puffing, she chewed her short, yellowed fingernails shorter. It made Emily nervous just to watch her.

"I still don't understand what you want with me." Emily coughed and tried not to tug at the ropes that held her wrists together behind the chair. The knots had already rubbed her skin raw as she had tried to get free.

"Something wrong? You look ill."

"I can't breathe, obviously." Emily could hardly see the woman behind her smoky veil. It stung every time she tried to take a breath.

"All right, then, girl, I'll—"

"Emily," Emily interrupted. She was tired of hearing "girl," tired of ropes, tired of smoke. It was more than she could take after just an afternoon.

Rivkah stared at Emily. The smoke curled about the table like a poisonous snake.

"My name isn't 'girl,' " continued Emily, wishing she could hold her breath. "It's Emily. And I insist you release me this moment."

A car honked out on the street, muffled and out of reach beyond the stained, dark shades and locked doors. At least Levi wasn't around. He had disappeared to a room down the hall.

"Emily, is it?" The woman smiled just enough to twitch the edges of her lips up, and then only for a second. She snuffed her cigarette in a blue bowl. "I suppose it doesn't matter if you know my name. I'm Rivkah."

"I know."

"Of course you do. You're a clever girl. Impertinent, but clever."

Emily made no move to answer. *Let her do and say what she will. Daddy will rescue me.* Or so she hoped—and prayed.

"Now, as I was about to say—" Rivkah coughed. "You want to write your parents a note, don't you?"

What is her point? Why does she want me to do that?

"You should tell them you're all right. That we're treating you well."

"Why don't *you* write the note?" Emily wiggled her arms. "You sound as if you know precisely what you want me to say."

Rivkah shrugged and pushed her chair out from the table. "It's up to you. I can tell them, or you can. I just thought your parents would want to know you aren't dead."

The words made Emily catch her breath. Her lip quivered. Of course Mum and Daddy were hurting, thinking she had drowned. Emily tried not to imagine what they were going through. But no, she could not give in to Rivkah. They would not want her to. God would not want her to. Whatever she could throw back at this horrid woman, she would.

"What do you need, money?" Emily blurted. She'd read a Dickens novel once where Fagin had tried to collect a ransom. *David Copperfield*, or was it *Oliver Twist*?

The woman leaned forward, her eyes locking on to Emily's.

"We don't need *English* money. We don't need English anything. We only work for what is rightfully ours, and now for the freedom of our Irgun comrade."

Irgun. The word stung Emily like a bee. So Rivkah and Levi were Irgun, the Jewish terrorists her father was always working so hard to capture. The ones who bragged about setting bombs in their messy war against the British, even setting them in places like her father's army offices in Jerusalem's beautiful King David …

Suddenly Emily's mind cleared, and she remembered what Rivkah had said in the jeep. It had seemed like an odd comment at the time.

"I didn't fail you at the King David . . ."

So Levi and Rivkah had been a part of that. Dozens of innocent people had been killed; Daddy had almost been one of them. But what could they possibly want from Emily? What could they possibly hope to gain?

"Did you hear me? It's time to write the note."

Emily stiffened. How could she write such a thing? Whatever Rivkah wanted couldn't be right.

But Rivkah went on. "Tell them you're alive and feeling fine."

Alive, perhaps. But feeling fine? Certainly not.

Rivkah pulled a pad of paper and a pencil from the far side of the table and pushed it toward Emily.

"And do you propose that I write it with a pencil in my mouth?" asked Emily.

"I'll untie you. First write your hello, then that you will be set free as soon as our Irgun comrade is released from Acre Prison. His name is Yehuda."

Emily felt her stomach go sour. A trade. One for one. Her freedom for the freedom of a criminal, a terrorist.

"I won't do it."

"Foolish girl. You think you're better than Yehuda, is that it?"

"I didn't say that." Emily couldn't keep the hot, angry tears from her eyes.

Rivkah hit the paper with her fist. "You help us, and you walk out of here. No one is hurt. You understand?"

Emily understood how easy it would be to say yes, to betray all her father worked for so she could be safe. How easy, and how horrible. Of course, it was tempting, but was it the right thing to do? Would her father's men ever forgive her?

"No." Emily stuck out her chin. "Absolutely not."

They stared at each other for a long minute, and Rivkah frowned and reached once more for her crushed cigarette as the sound of Levi's heavy footsteps came down the hallway.

"Oh, you'll change your mind soon enough," she assured her with a cold look.

Emily shivered at the thought that Rivkah might be right.

TEMPTATION

11

"Hamburgers! Who'da thought?" Stan Loftin wasn't the only American visitor enjoying himself at the kibbutz dinner the next evening, a full day after the visitors had arrived. The big American's booming voice filled the dining hall. "All we've had so far in this country are salads—you know, rabbit food?"

"Mmm." Henrik nodded and wiped the juice off his chin. A tomato slipped out and fell onto his plate.

"Never tasted better, even back home," Stan continued. "But where do you get your fresh beef out here on the kye-byoots?"

Henrik choked back a piece of meat, smiled, and carefully carved another bite with his knife and fork.

"We have our ways" was all Henrik would say. Finally the young Dane excused himself and made his way over to where Dov was sitting, as far away from Henrik as he could.

"Dov, are you all right down here? Why don't you sit with us?"

"I'm not hungry," Dov mumbled into his plate without looking up. He wasn't.

"Oh. Well, I want you to know that no one blames you for...you know."

Dov knew. *Please don't mention the dead cow.* No matter the danger, the men of the kibbutz had dragged it back after dark last night. Dov pushed the meat around on his plate some more.

"Everyone likes the hamburger steaks." Henrik must have been trying his best, but he was trying *too* hard. "They're quite good, a little like my mother used to make in Denmark. Right, Mom?" He looked to his mother, who sat chatting at the next table with a few of her women friends. She looked up and smiled, and he went on.

"They were delicious with some brown onion sauce. Very kosher, I think."

Dov pushed his metal army plate away with enough force that it clattered to the floor. He hadn't wanted to do that.

Everyone around him hushed and stared at the mess on the wood plank floor.

"I don't need you to feel sorry for me," mumbled Dov. "I just need to leave!"

"Sure, Dov." Henrik stooped to pick up the plate, and they bumped heads. "Ouch! Here, let me help you. . . ."

That was all Dov could take of people watching him and feeling sorry for him. He ran from the dining hall as fast as he could, stumbled down the steps and out into the night, out to where he could catch his breath and think.

Why not leave this kibbutz right now? He wasn't afraid of any Arabs with their guns. He wasn't scared of anyone. Dov stopped short and felt the warm night breeze on his cheek. He could smell the tinge of salt carried over the hills from the ocean he could not see.

"I'm sorry Emily left without saying good-bye, too." Henrik

had followed him. "But you know the soldiers who came for her were in a hurry."

Dov didn't answer. He, too, had heard what the kibbutz gatekeeper reported at dinner last night.

"That's what's *really* bothering you, isn't it? That she left?"

"No!"

Dov spun to face Henrik, his fists at his side. But instead of hitting him, Dov ran.

Dov wasn't sure where he was going—anyplace away from Henrik and the others. When he tired of running, he walked, trying to decide the best way to escape the kibbutz without being seen. He noticed a light flickering from under the door of the hen house, then heard a voice inside. He stepped closer and stopped to listen.

"I tell you, no one's going to find this girl in Ashkelon. Levi and Rivkah have things under control. But something had better happen soon. Is the note ready?"

Someone mumbled in response, though not clearly enough that Dov could hear the answer.

"Well, find out!"

The mumbler mumbled something else before he threw the door open in Dov's face.

"What are you doing here?" barked the young man. He was one of Moshe's kibbutz "soldiers" who practiced with the broomstick "rifles."

"I was just—" Dov turned to leave.

"Come in here, kid!" Moshe's order was hard to ignore. Dov could have run, but the leash of a voice held him in place. Yet if there was one person Dov did *not* want to see just then, it was Moshe Cohen.

"I said, come here." Dov turned but kept one foot out the door, just in case. He would hear what Moshe had to say.

The mumbler wasn't happy but left them without a word.

"I heard what you did yesterday. I like your spirit." Moshe hardly looked up from where he sat on a sack of feed, cleaning a rifle with a rag.

Dov didn't answer. He surely didn't know what Moshe was talking about. Moshe liked something about *him*?

"I like your *chutzpah*. Your fight. Taking on a barbed-wire fence."

"Oh." *That.*

"You're mad at the world, right?"

Dov wasn't about to be pulled into a conversation.

"You can't hide it from me, kid. I am, too."

"So?"

"So I could show you how to take on something more interesting than wire fences. Like the Arabs, or the English. Do you understand what I'm saying?"

"No."

Moshe sighed.

"I think you do—what's the name…Dov?"

Dov nodded. Moshe had gotten *that* right.

"Well, Dov, we're always looking for people like you."

"We?"

"That's right." Moshe didn't really answer Dov's question. "And you need something to do, something better than collecting eggs, right?"

"All I need is to go to Jerusalem to find my family."

"I could help you do that."

Dov's heart almost stopped. Could Moshe really help?

"Why do you act so surprised? You help me, I help you. That's just the way we do things."

"I don't help anyone," began Dov, lowering his voice to sound a little older, a little tougher.

But Moshe only smiled.

"Perfect. We can work with a fellow like you."

We again. It reminded Dov that he still had no clear idea who Moshe really was. After what Henrik had said, he wasn't sure if he wanted to know. But if Moshe could help Dov find his family, maybe that was all that mattered.

"Don't stand there like a tree, Dov. Come here and take this. I'll show you. You're not one of them. You never will be."

By this time the young people had lit a bonfire in the middle of the kibbutz plaza, and in the distance Dov could see the girls were taking the lead in another hora dance. It looked as if the Americans were eager to join in, and they had all joined hands in the dancing and laughing.

"Did you hear me, Dov? You're not one of them."

Moshe held out a rifle to him. "Here. First I'll show you how to clean one of these. Learn to shoot, and in a few months maybe you can graduate to better things." He chuckled, and Dov wasn't sure what "better things" might mean.

Dov slowly reached out to take the weapon. It was heavier than he thought. Colder too.

"What'd you come out here for, anyway?" Moshe asked. "Steal some eggs? Look for your girlfriend?"

"She's no girlfriend of mine!" snapped Dov.

"Of course not. That's why your ears are all red."

Dov didn't like the way Moshe teased, his less-than-friendly grin. Dov didn't like the gun, either—he had never liked them. Guns reminded him of the camps, of Nazis, of war.

But no one had ever asked Dov to help, not quite like this. A part of him wanted to say yes right away, to join something bigger than himself. He wanted to *belong*.

Moshe laughed. "Don't worry about it. The English girl is fine."

"What do you know about Emily?" Dov wasn't sure why he asked, but how would Moshe know?

Moshe's eyes narrowed, and he stared straight at Dov. And though Dov desperately wanted to, he could not look away.

"You know as much as I do. British soldiers came yesterday afternoon to take her home. Am I not right?"

"Yes."

"So. Let me show you this rifle."

I can't do this. Can I? "I, ah…I don't know. Let me think about it."

"Sure, think all you want. And while you're thinking, the British are bleeding us dry. The Arabs are circling like vultures. We're the only ones—"

"We, we, we!" Dov blurted out. "Who *are* you talking about? Henrik says—"

"Henrik's an idiot!" Moshe's eyes blazed. "But I'll promise you one thing. You help me, and I'll make sure you find out everything you need to know about us…in time. I—"

Moshe stopped short when the shed door squeaked open.

"Oh, there you are, Dov," said the newcomer. "I was just wondering …" Henrik's voice trailed off when Dov turned around, rifle in hand.

Henrik looked as if he had been slapped in the face. "Dov," he gasped. "What are you *doing* with that thing?"

Dov looked from Henrik and back to Moshe. What *was* he doing?

"We're just talking about working together." Moshe put out his hands, palms up. "Nothing that concerns you."

"Put it down, Dov." Henrik ignored Moshe and pointed at the rifle.

"It's not loaded," said Moshe, "if *that's* what you're worried about. You wouldn't be afraid of an empty gun, now, would you?"

Henrik kept his eyes on Dov. "Just put it down, and let's get out of here, Dov. Please."

"He's a big boy, Henrik. Maybe he's tired of all that peace rubbish you've been feeding him."

For a moment Dov wrestled with belonging, and Moshe's promises.

Henrik tried one more time. "Come on, Dov. You don't want to do this. Just put the gun down."

"Listen to him. Doesn't he sound dangerous?" Moshe smirked.

Dov hesitated. The dancing and singing had stopped outside, and the sudden quiet caught his attention.

Even Moshe looked over Dov's shoulder, and he stiffened. "What?" He ran to the door and looked outside.

"Give me that." Henrik grabbed the gun from Dov, then turned to see what Moshe was so worried about.

"What happened to our warning?" asked Moshe, holding the door shut. "They're back again!"

In an instant Moshe's face had changed from hunter to hunted. Dov saw the reason when he peeked outside himself: two British soldiers, talking to the bonfire crowd from the seats of their jeep.

"I wasn't here. You understand?" Moshe grabbed Henrik's collar, a nose-to-nose warning. "You may be an idiot, but you're still a Jew."

He turned to the shadows, scattering a couple of squawking hens, and disappeared.

✡ ✡ ✡

Levi seemed pleased, and even Rivkah had stopped smoking long enough to smile at the note.

"Lovely." He beamed and waved the paper in Emily's face as he read. " 'Dear Mum and Daddy. Please don't worry about me. I am alive and being held. I can't tell you the exact place. They have not harmed me, but they want me to tell you that they will not let me go until the British release their friend Yehuda from Acre Prison. They have guns, and they're serious. I love you. Your loving daughter, Emily.' "

Emily hung her head. She had not wanted to write the note, but she could not stand up to Levi the way she had stood up to Rivkah.

Forgive me, she prayed silently.

"All right, Levi, you have the note." Rivkah tried to take it, but he held the paper out of reach.

"Yes." Levi laughed. Then his face turned serious. "Maybe when they read this, these ignorant British will finally realize whose country they occupy. The tougher we show them we are, the sooner they'll leave. Does it say 'an eye for an eye' in your Bible, English girl?"

Please help me out of this, Lord. Emily rested her forehead on the table and didn't answer.

"Oh, the sweet young girl is tired after so much work." Levi stroked the dark shadow of beard on his face. "Rivkah, why don't you give her something to drink?"

Emily sat up straight and shook her head. She had an idea. "Nothing to drink, thank you. I just need to use the WC."

"But of course," Levi told her as he again untied her ropes. "We're perfectly reasonable. You can tell your father that.

"In fact, we brought you to one of the nicest homes in the city, didn't we, Rivkah? Most of the other homes in this neighborhood have only an outhouse. But it wouldn't do to have our honored guest living in such primitive conditions, now, would it?"

An outhouse would have been just fine with Emily, but she stumbled into the dark bathroom. From what she knew of Ashkelon, the seaside town wasn't as modern as Tel Aviv or the New City of Jerusalem. It was known mostly for its ancient ruins, where the Canaanites and the Philistines had lived thousands of years ago. But in its day this row house must have been quite fancy, one of the few homes to have indoor plumbing—although the bathroom hadn't been cleaned since Samson's day, she thought. She wrinkled her nose at the smell.

"Hurry up, now!" Levi warned her.

Emily closed the door behind her and tugged at the string to turn on a bare light bulb hanging in the middle of the room. Her wrists tingled as she rubbed them to help the blood return to her hands, her eyes quickly taking in what little the room had to offer.

There it was. The window.

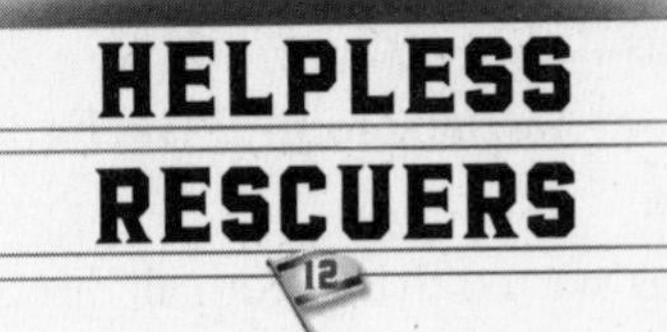

HELPLESS RESCUERS

"Quiet. *Quiet!*" One of the kibbutz elders, a tall man named Ruben, raised his hands and his voice to make himself heard over the hubbub. "One at a time, please! Dov, will you explain what you saw and heard? You're the only one who seems to know what has happened."

Dov didn't know everything—just much more than he wanted to know.

He glanced over at Henrik's mother, who still dabbed at the corner of her eyes with a kerchief. Perhaps it would have been good if Matthias were there right now to help straighten out this terrible mess.

"Speak up, young man," Ruben demanded. "It worries us when British soldiers come searching our kibbutz so often. We must know your part in this."

"Dov couldn't help it," Henrik began, but Ruben wanted to hear from Dov, not him.

Dov cleared his throat and traced a circle in the dust with the toe of his shoe. Now he *really* wished he had jumped the fence yesterday, maybe even said yes to Moshe just to get out of the kibbutz. Anything. Facing angry Arabs seemed better than this.

"I, ah…that is …"

"Did Moshe say anything to you? Did he say where he was going?"

The questions started flying from all directions.

"Moshe ran out the back of the chicken coop as soon as he saw the British soldiers," Dov finally explained. "He disappeared. That's all I can tell you."

"But why were you talking to Moshe?" Ruben asked. "And why did the soldiers push Henrik around?"

"It's really not his fault," Henrik said. "Dov was just—"

Ruben held up his hand. "Let the young man speak for himself, Henrik."

"I just don't understand why the soldiers thought Henrik was doing anything wrong," said Henrik's mother.

Dov had to say it. "Perhaps because he was holding Moshe's gun when they saw us."

"Ohh." Ruben put his hand to his forehead and groaned. "And you, Henrik, of all people."

"Henrik was just trying to take it away from me." Dov didn't know what else to say. It was *his* fault, really. If he hadn't stopped to talk to Moshe, Henrik wouldn't have followed him, and if he hadn't been holding Moshe's gun, Henrik wouldn't have taken it from him. Never mind that the gun was legal—sort of.

But there was something else about tonight that didn't make sense.

"What I don't understand is why the soldiers came back." Ruben said what Dov was thinking. "Especially when soldiers had already come to get the English girl yesterday. She has something to do with all this, too."

"Yeah, something's not right about all this." Stan Loftin stepped up to the fire.

"It could be the soldiers are confused," someone suggested.

"Could be." Stan shook his head. "But I don't think so. You see, I talked to them myself, and they told me that Emily's father, Major Parkinson, just heard today about her being found here."

The crowd buzzed at Stan's words and at the on-the-spot translation for those who didn't understand English. But no one seemed to have any answers. Only questions.

"He would have come himself for his girl, they tell me, only he's in the middle of some kind of big search for Jewish terrorists."

More buzzing.

"They told you this?" asked Ruben.

Stan nodded and continued. "So what are the facts here? The English girl disappears without a word yesterday; then another couple of Brits come to get her today, direct from her dad, and *they* think she's still *here*. That doesn't make any sense. There's something wrong here.

"Dov." The American swiveled to stare at him. "Can you remember anything else? *Anything* Moshe might have said? From what you tell me about this man, I think he knows more than he let on. After all, why else would he have told you that Emily was fine?"

Dov had already squeezed his memory dry. But what about the fellow Moshe had been talking to when Dov walked up to the chicken house? He was gone now, of course. Nowhere to be found. That was strange, too.

"Moshe and his friend—the one who disappeared when I walked up—were just talking about girls, or ..." Dov realized what he was saying. "A girl. Wait a minute, they were talking about a *girl*!"

"Who?" Stan jumped on the question, a dog on a bone.

"Wait, wait . . ." Dov squeezed his head. "Rachel, I think. No, *Rivkah*. And a man, too—Levi."

"Do you know any Levis or Rivkahs?" Stan looked around at the others, but their blank looks said no. "All right. What else?"

Dov shook his head. That was all he could remember.

"All right," the American told them. "This is a good start. We don't know where Moshe is, but maybe this Levi and Rivkah will. Actually, I think if we can just find Moshe, we'll find your English friend."

"I told you not to lock the door!" Levi rattled the bathroom door while Emily kicked the handle on the toilet tank once more, just for effect. She had been standing on the seat, trying to pry the window boards loose, but it was no use. After two days of trying to loosen it every chance she got, she was certain the window was nailed shut from both the inside and out and wouldn't budge. Levi and Rivkah had thought of everything.

"I just need a bit of privacy," Emily called back. "And I shall lock the door whenever I please."

"Rivkah, what is she *doing* in there?" Levi wanted to know.

She wiggled the boards back and forth one more time. Standing on her tiptoes, Emily *was* finally able to get a peek out at the dusty Ashkelon street. An old man on a donkey ambled past in the early morning sun. Perhaps she could drop a note through, maybe on a piece of paper. If only she had taken the pencil along with her.

"Out! Now!" threatened Rivkah, pounding even harder on the door.

"I'm not feeling well," answered Emily, which was true. Her head had felt better, much better.

"Tell her I don't care *how* ill she says she is, she's coming out of there right now."

"Levi says …"

Emily heard what Levi said, and she expected the angry man to come crashing through the bathroom door any minute. She took one more quick peek at freedom before she pulled the toilet handle one last time, stepped down off the toilet, and unlocked the door.

She put a hand on her stomach and gave a glaring Rivkah her best show. "I'm sorry," croaked Emily. "I'm quite ill. You've been holding me here for two days."

"Well, don't blame it on the food." Levi wagged a finger at her. "And don't you lock that door again."

"It's what I'm used to doing," Emily squeaked. "Just a habit."

"Yeah," Levi grumbled and headed for the back door, then turned to Rivkah. "Well, I'm going to check on Moshe to see if he's heard anything. It shouldn't take long."

"But, Levi," Rivkah replied, "we only just delivered the note last night."

Levi looked at his wristwatch. "Yes, and what time is it now? Eight-thirty in the morning already."

"Thank you, I can tell time. But we gave them until four o'clock this afternoon to agree to our demands. Eight o'clock tomorrow morning to set Yehuda free."

"Sure, sure, but where's Moshe? Sitting out on a street corner playing dominoes? He needs to tell us what the British say. And we'll need some time to prepare for the exchange."

"Fine, then. Go sit in a café with Moshe and leave me here."

"Calm down, Rivkah! I'll find Moshe, all right? Be right back." Levi didn't bother to tuck in his shirt and slammed the door behind him.

Emily sighed with relief. Now she would only have to face Rivkah.

"I still don't think it's a good idea for you to leave now." Henrik stood with his arms crossed watching the Americans pack up their car. "You've been here only a day and two nights. It's not safe on the roads."

"I appreciate what you're saying, but the roads were no better when we came." Stan's voice drifted out from underneath the Model A; all Dov could see were his enormous feet. "Could somebody hand me that wrench again?"

Dov slid the tool in as close as he could.

"And what about Dov?" Henrik didn't sound as if he was going to drop the subject. "He's—"

"He's old enough to make up his own mind," Stan finished the sentence. "He wants to go to Jerusalem, and we're happy to give him a ride."

"I'm just worried that you won't make it."

"The old Model A's in great shape." Stan crawled out like an enormous inchworm, got to his feet, and dusted himself off. "My uncle Gerald did business in Beirut, had it shipped over brand-new from the States in '29. But he hardly ever used it, and then my aunt Lynne—"

"Uh, Stan . . ." Chip shifted from foot to foot. "I don't think they want to hear the whole story."

"Okay, I can get carried away, I know." Stan shrugged and looked around at the group. "Well, ready to pray?"

Uh-oh. Dov inched his way backward but Stan caught him.

"Oh no, you don't, kid," he said. "You travel with us, you pray with us, too."

Dov was caught, so he listened to the Americans pray. He had to admit they sounded different when they talked to God—nothing like the gum-chewing, bubble-popping "hey you's" they tossed at each other. There was a quiet respect he'd never heard before, and the words they used were their own.

"Father, I pray for Emily's safety, for Stan and Chip, Les and Clarence...and Dov," Henrik prayed, too.

Dov squirmed but could not free himself from Stan's gentle grip. The big American had locked his arm around Dov's shoulder. Dov might have been embarrassed, but everyone else's eyes were closed, all heads bowed.

"I pray also that thou would hold them and keep them on the way of peace," Henrik finished, "for I pray in the name of *HaMashiach*, the Messiah. Amen."

"Amen," echoed the Americans. They had barely opened their eyes when Stan turned the key and the trusty Model A roared to life.

"What did I tell you?" Stan said. "It'll be like a ride on the Pennsylvania Turnpike."

"I don't think—" began Henrik, but Stan held up his hand.

"You've been good to us," he told Henrik, resting his hands on the boy's shoulders, "and I thank you. Don't worry."

Finally Henrik returned the smile. "You just take care of Dov for me, will you?" He turned to Dov. "I mean what I said earlier." He shook Dov's hand. "You have to promise to come back and visit. Soon."

Dov nodded.

"I just wish we knew where to look for your friend Emily," Stan said from the driver's seat. "I feel really bad about what might have happened to her."

Henrik looked away, and Dov understood his concern. What could anyone say?

Dov found a seat by the window, behind the driver. Chip rode up front with Stan, Les shared the middle seat with Dov, and Clarence had the third seat all to himself.

"All right, up to Jerusalem!" said Stan. "Ready, Dov?"

Dov felt the Magen David poke him in the leg. A thought came to him.

"Here, wait a minute." Dov dug the necklace out of his pocket. He held it out the window to Henrik.

"Here, you should have this. It means more to you than it does to me."

Henrik looked down for a second and put his hand over the top of Dov's, but he didn't take the gift.

"Thank you, Dov, but you need to keep it. I hope it will mean something to you, too, someday."

Dov took the necklace back, wondering. *I tried.*

Soon the Model A was bouncing down the lane, the kibbutz kids running alongside. Dov recognized a couple of the Russian children who had hidden with him in the well. He waved, and they shouted something back to him he didn't understand.

"Remember!" Henrik called after him. "You come back. You promised!"

Dov sat with the Magen David in his lap and tried not to look back at the kibbutz. This was surely *not* the way he'd wanted to leave. He thought again that he should have slipped out on his own, before all these Americans had come and complicated things. Why was life always so complicated, anyway? And why had Emily gone and probably gotten herself kidnapped? Things would have been much easier if she hadn't done that.

Stan leaned on the horn as they eased away from the waving crowd. "Anyone know the fastest way to Jerusalem?"

THE ATTACK

13

Up to Jerusalem!

Dov knew he should be excited to finally be headed in the right direction. At last he was going to find Imma and Abba, or at least he would be closer to them than in years. He ought to be thinking of how to find his family instead of worrying about Emily. She would take care of herself—or her father would.

But he couldn't stop trying to remember the conversation he'd heard back at Yad Shalom the night before. Rivkah, Levi, and…what else? Nothing new came to him; it was a sealed box he could not open. Rivkah. A girl. They're safe…she's safe in …?

Is there more to remember?

He gave up and stared ahead as they bumped down the coastal road through a lonely stretch of sand dunes. So far that morning, no Arab mobs had attacked them. Stan had steered around some of the Arab towns out of caution. Chip fiddled with a map in the front seat, trying to unfold it, holding it up close to his face to see. "Do you know where we are, Les?"

He was holding the map upside down. "Seems to me we've been going in circles."

"Here." Dov leaned over and turned the map around for the American. He liked maps; they reminded him of the charts he used to look at when he was on the *Aliyah*. He could see the beach in the north where he and Emily had landed, the spot where the refugees were supposed to have come ashore. He pointed to the road he thought they were traveling and put his finger on the coastal road, just north of …

He leaned over the seat, closer to the bouncing map, and focused on the little dot of a city.

"I tell you, no one's going to find this girl in Ashkelon."

That's what Moshe had said! *Ashkelon*, just south of them on the coast. Of course!

Dov grabbed the map out of Chip's hands, just to make sure.

"Hey!" Chip tried to take it back. "I was doing fine."

"Turn right up here," ordered Dov. He held the map out of Chip's reach.

The others look at him oddly.

"What?" Stan looked confused.

"Turn right, I said!"

"That road will take us to Ashkelon." Chip could see the sign ahead, its lettering in English and Arabic and Hebrew. "We're not going to Ashkelon."

"We are now," replied Dov. Quickly he explained what he had finally remembered.

Stan whooped from the driver's seat and pounded the wheel. "Let's go find your friend, Dov!"

"She's not …" Dov gave up explaining and concentrated on the task ahead. He wasn't sure how big of a place Ashkelon was, and he had no idea what they would do when they got there—or even what they would do if they somehow found the missing Emily Parkinson.

✡ ✡ ✡

Eleven-thirty, only a few more hours until the deadline Levi had set for the British to agree to their demands. Four and a half hours, to be exact. Emily could hear the wall clock ticking the minutes.

She read and reread the front page of the newspaper sitting in front of her on the unsteady kitchen table, articles she would normally never have paid much attention to: another Jewish refugee ship stopped and taken to Haifa. Barclay's Bank robbed in Jerusalem. Even the ads: *Discriminating women will always prefer Elizabeth Arden's preparations, obtainable at the New Jerusalem Pharmacy on Zion Cinema Street.*

She counted flies on the rose wallpaper, and did her best, with her hands still tied, to keep a particularly fat one from landing on her nose. She listened, too, for noises out on the street, but if there was anything to hear, it didn't travel through the walls of the house.

"You know," said Rivkah in between puffs on her ever present cigarette, "I'm not such a bad person when you get to know me."

Emily wiggled her wrists and thought how she might answer. What could she say to convince Rivkah to loosen the ropes just a little more? Her right hand was starting to fall asleep again.

Rivkah studied the ceiling as she talked. "You have brothers, sisters?" she asked. It seemed like a peculiar time for small talk. Emily would rather read the Hassneh Insurance Company of Palestine ad. But in the end her manners won out. She shook her head politely.

"It's just me and Julian."

"Your brother?"

"Our dog. He's a Great Dane."

"I had a dog when I was young." Rivkah actually smiled, and her voice softened. "Or actually, the neighbor in our apartment building had a dog. My little sister, Anna, and I took care of him. Took him for walks around Tel Aviv, made him pull my doll carriage—before my father died and we had to move to live with my aunt in Jerusalem. In fact…you look quite a lot like my sister."

She looked curiously at Emily, as if seeing her for the first time.

Emily glanced away. She had felt nearly as uncomfortable when her father once insisted she sit for a portrait. Where to look?

"Are you all right?" asked Rivkah. "You're not getting sick, are you?"

"I'll feel much better when you let me go, thank you." Emily yawned and wondered if she would ever sleep in her own bed again instead of this hard chair. It would be wonderful, too, to taste Ginger's cooking rather than the bland cheese and bread Rivkah had been feeding her. For now the best she could hope to do was scratch her back, just behind her right shoulder. She tried to slouch to rub against the back of the chair, but it didn't work. She certainly wasn't going to ask Rivkah for help.

"It all depends on your father now." Rivkah sighed. "If he cooperates, you could be eating breakfast at home tomorrow morning."

Tomorrow morning … Yes, Daddy would make sure she was okay, but she didn't think he would want to deal with these people—not the way they wanted to deal.

"You may not believe this," Rivkah said, "but I'm sorry things turned out this way. No one ever told me you were going to be so young."

What else are you sorry for? Emily silently asked. Was she supposed to thank her captor for feeling sorry? What if she and Levi didn't do as they promised? Or what if, heaven forbid, they didn't let her go at all? Emily closed her eyes to pray, to think. What if she couldn't escape through the bathroom window? For the first time her stomach really *did* hurt, and it only got worse.

"Are you sure you're well?" Rivkah asked. She seemed to Emily more worried about what she might have to clean up than worried about how Emily felt.

"Yes, I mean, no, my stomach feels...quite awful."

Emily wondered how much it would take to convince Rivkah she needed a doctor, someone she could signal for help. After all, her stomach *did* hurt. Maybe it would help if it hurt more. She lowered her forehead to the table and sighed.

"My stomach ..." Emily barely whispered her complaint, so Rivkah had to lean forward to hear. "It feels as if it's going to burst."

Bam!

Dov nearly jumped through the ceiling of the Model A. For a second he thought the noise was Clarence in the backseat again, blowing up and popping the paper sack they had used to pack their lunches.

"That's not funny!" Dov complained. "It sounds as if someone is shooting—"

Dov didn't finish as the old Ford jolted sideways and Stan wrestled with the big black steering wheel.

"No joke!" he told them through gritted teeth. They wobbled dangerously over a dozen potholes before they again heard the loud popping outside.

Pop-pop-pop! One of the pops smashed into the wooden side of the car with a sickening thud.

Dov knew exactly what was happening. "Everybody down!" he cried. "Someone's shooting at us!"

Les yelled, almost screamed, but they did as they were told. Stan was the only one with his head up, and he was doing his best to keep them on the road.

"We have to stop!" Chip yelled.

Thunk-ka, thunk-ka. A tire flapped uselessly, but they drove on as fast as they dared, everyone shouting advice at once.

"Stop? Are you crazy?" Stan still gripped the wheel. "We can't stop here."

"Keep driving," Les cried. "We need to get out of here."

Ka-thunk, ka-thunk.

"That's right," Clarence agreed. "Keep going."

"But we're going to *crash*!" yelled Chip.

"No!"

It was good for them that Stan seemed to keep his cool during all the screaming.

"Duck your head and pray!" Stan roared, ducking himself as he kept one hand on the wheel.

Another round of *pop-pop*s. With their car's long wooden sides, Dov was sure they gave the attacker a large target. Now every member of the North Philadelphia Young All-Church Council Holyland '47 Goodwill Tour was on his knees in the bottom of the car, elbow to elbow. Except for Stan, of course.

"Our Father," prayed the Americans, and Dov silently repeated the unfamiliar words after them.

A little prayer can't hurt at a time like this.

✡ ✡ ✡

"You did what?" Levi's ears were red with fury. "What kind of softheaded idiotic idea was that, bringing in a *doctor* for this prisoner? And so close to the deadline?"

"Listen, Levi." Rivkah licked her lips and locked the door behind her partner. "Nothing happened, all right? I thought it was something serious. What good would it do us if she died?"

"Bah!" Levi pulled Emily's head up and looked her over quickly, as though she were a melon in the market. At least he didn't thump her with his knuckles. "She's fine. I could have told you that. And if we don't hear from her father soon, a stomachache's going to be the least of her problems."

The least of my problems? Emily didn't like the sound of that.

"That's what I *mean*, Levi." Rivkah was nearly pleading with the man. "I didn't want things to go wrong after all this trouble. I had to make a decision."

"Yeah? Well, from now on, you let *me* make those kinds of decisions."

"You weren't here."

Emily kept as still as she could, wishing she were invisible.

"Use your head, Rivkah. Think what could have happened."

Nothing did happen, thought Emily, wishing desperately that it had. She'd thought of slipping a note to the old doctor, or even making a scene, but there was never a chance. Rivkah had been watching every second, her gun pointed at Emily from under a knitted shawl.

The man had simply poked Emily in the stomach a couple

of times and given her a blue bottle full of horrible-tasting chalk to drink. She figured the chalk was almost worse than the stomachache.

"Nothing happened, Levi." Rivkah crossed her arms. "The old man didn't even notice her wrists were red from the ropes. He was half asleep. Stop worrying about nothing."

" 'Nothing,' she says. You bring in an old doctor to coddle this girl, and you say it's nothing. What did you pay him with, anyway?"

Rivkah smiled, but it was a cold smile. "Your stash of money for emergencies, remember?"

"But that was *mine*!

"Not anymore. I gave him a little extra, just to make sure he doesn't go around town sharing what he saw."

"You're beginning to make me sorry I brought you along on this job."

"Well, it's too late for that. And nothing's going to happen. Quit worrying, all right?"

"I'm going out to see Moshe again and find out if Parkinson has responded yet," he told them. "But this time, see that you keep any visitors out. Don't answer the door unless it's me. Understand?"

Rivkah waved him off like a pesky fly. "Just leave us alone, Levi. I can take care of things myself!"

"Women!" Levi grumbled and slammed the front door behind him.

"Men!" she hissed in return.

DISCOVERED

14

Two miles farther down the road, Dov was sure they couldn't go on. But then, he had been sure of the same thing two miles before that. The tire was ruined, of course, and the wheel probably looked like a warped bagel, too. And the horrible noise!

"Look at that!" Dov peeked out the window to report on their progress. "The rim's making sparks, hitting rocks." His teeth rattled to the rhythm of the bent wheel rim on the rough road.

"Keep inside and stay down, Dov!" Stan cried, but Dov had already seen all he needed to. None of the other tour members had raised their heads.

"I think we're clear," Dov reassured them. He didn't see anything unusual outside the car now, aside from the fireworks display from the back left wheel. But what should he have been looking for? A sharpshooter in full *kaffiyeh*—an Arab man's headdress, held in place by a thick cord around the top of the head?

"Woo!" Chip stomped his feet and clapped his hands. "That

was a close one, eh? We're keeping our guardian angels working overtime."

"Yeah, good job, Stan!" Les and Clarence smiled and slapped their driver on the back.

Dov wondered how Stan had kept the car going. He was sure by now he'd never met people like this before. *Someone shoots at their car, and what do they do? Pray.* Ten minutes later they were smiling and patting each other on the back as if they had just won some kind of game. Crazy, crazy Americans!

"I think we can pull over here, Stan." Chip pointed out a wide spot in the road up ahead in a hollow between two low hills.

Stan was driving too fast, or maybe he didn't see how close the ditch was to their ruined back left tire. And he surely didn't realize how deep it was, or he wouldn't have edged the Ford so close to the side of the road. Whatever happened, they slid to the left as solid ground crumbled beneath them. Everyone inside the leaning Model A tumbled over one another in a slow-motion heap.

"Hold on!" Stan yelled.

Here we go. Dov dug his fingernails into the seat, waiting for the car to turn upside down.

It never happened, not quite. The slow-motion slide backward finally stopped, and Dov looked around. In the stunned silence all he could hear was the escaping steam from their radiator.

"Ohh!" Emily tried to make the most horrific, pained sounds she knew, each time louder than the last. She guessed that the louder she made them, the less Rivkah would want to come in and help. It really wasn't hard to imagine that her stomachache had turned into something horrible and painful.

"Oooh, oh, oh!" Emily turned on the faucet with her foot, reached up, and tugged once more at the corner of the boards covering her only way to freedom. Even if the window were wide open, though, it would be tough to crawl through. It would be a tight fit, too tight for an adult with big shoulders. But for Emily...perhaps if she turned sideways and wiggled ... It was her only hope.

"You sound as if you're dying in there." Rivkah's voice was muffled, maybe even a little concerned. "Didn't the doctor help?"

Good. Rivkah could hear Emily's sick-to-her-stomach act. Once more, then, for good measure.

"Ohh, yes, a bit. But it still hurts. Ugh, oh!"

If it weren't so serious—and if she hadn't felt so guilty for making it all up—Emily's act would almost have been fun. The board she tugged at moved a little, then a little more. Perhaps she *could* manage. The trick was to time her "ugh's" and "ohh no's" to cover the squeaks of the boards. Rivkah must not suspect anything, nor Levi. Especially not him. He could be back anytime.

There! The board finally swung away far enough that she could see the street and people walking about in the early afternoon. Pity she couldn't pry it open more. It was so hard to see; she was peering through little more than a crack. Could she somehow get the attention of someone on the street? A few more tugs, and—

"Feeling better?"

Emily froze. Rivkah's voice suddenly sounded much, much closer.

"Get down from there before I strangle you, you little

weasel. This is what I get for showing you some kindness?"

Rivkah, in fact, was standing just inches away, her hands on her hips. Emily must not have locked the door all the way.

"Uh, uh, you see …" Emily struggled for words. Finally, she put her nose up to the window and took a deep breath. "I was just trying to get some fresh air. I needed to … I believe all your smoke is making me more nauseous."

"Get down!" Rivkah wasn't believing a word of it. She grabbed at Emily's ankle, and Emily slipped to the dirty tile floor with a thud, crumpling at Rivkah's feet.

"Now, get back to the table. You're not leaving my sight for *anything* from now on. It's two-thirty, and for *your* sake you'd better hope we hear from your father very soon. Do you hear?"

Emily heard. She nodded and limped back to the kitchen table, Rivkah nipping at her heels.

✡ ✡ ✡

"Is everyone all right?" Stan asked as the Model A tottered in the roadside ditch.

"I…I think so." Chip unfolded himself from the top of the heap. "Sorry, Les."

"Your knee's in my ear, Clarence." Les pressed himself against the topside door, which he opened like a submarine hatch.

"Careful, now," Stan said as he helped them climb out to safety. They stared at the one-car wreck once everyone was standing out on the road. Fortunately, it didn't look smashed and undriveable—just stuck and tipped backward.

"Changing the tire wouldn't have been too difficult," Stan said. "But I don't know how we're going to get out of this ditch."

"Simple." Clarence looked as if he might try pulling the car out all by himself. Like his friend Les, though, he wasn't too big. "We all just pull the car out with a rope."

All the others groaned, and Dov walked away to let them discuss it. What was behind the hills that surrounded them? He checked the way they had come first to see if anyone had followed. Where was the person who had used their car for target practice? Then he walked ahead to the top of the rise to see if any traffic was coming toward them from the other direction.

"Don't wander off!" warned Stan.

That would not be a problem, thought Dov as he waved back at him; there was nowhere else to hide if someone should attack again. Did he hear something?

Dov shaded his eyes and looked off into the distance to see what was making the odd sound, coming closer and closer. Not a car, surely, or a truck or an army jeep. But a soft whistle, a "yah," a tinkle of bells.

"Someone's coming!" He turned around and ran back toward the group. Someone, he was sure, but just how many, and were they in danger?

Stan looked up from tying the end of a rope to the front bumper of the Ford.

"What? Who?"

"I don't know! I just heard whistling and bells. Might be a bunch of men."

"Soldiers?" Chip asked.

They gathered around the car, waiting for whoever it was to come over the crest of the slope. "Just stand still," Stan ordered. "I'll do the talking."

✡ ✡ ✡

Emily watched as Rivkah built up the cloud of smoke in the kitchen. Emily could only look away and wish she didn't have to breathe. Rivkah peeked out through the blind and paced, puffed, and paced, starting a new cigarette from the old one.

Whatever was out there, it was making Rivkah even more nervous than she had been before, if that was possible.

Rivkah paused from her smoking long enough to glance at her wristwatch for the tenth time. At least she had left Emily's ankles untied this time, so Emily could wiggle her feet and toes. Her arms were still tightly tied behind her back.

"Where *is* he?" Rivkah wondered aloud. It was true that Levi had been gone now for quite a while. One hour? Two? Finally Rivkah looked over at the telephone on its wall shelf, paused, and snapped her fingers.

"He thinks *he* can make all the decisions. Well, I've got news for him."

Emily wasn't sure she wanted to hear the news. But while Levi the cat was away, Rivkah the mouse was obviously up to something.

"While he's out there muddling around, I'm sitting here waiting." Rivkah paced furiously. "Well, I'll tell you something. I'm not going to let him tell me what to do anymore. I'm sick of waiting!"

Rivkah stepped over to the black phone and ripped the receiver off the wall cradle. It fell and dangled by the straight cord until she picked it back up.

"Hello?" she barked into the phone in English a minute later. Her voice sounded different, huskier, but she couldn't make herself sound like a man instead of a woman no matter how hard she tried. "Give me Major Porkinson—now. No, you get him right now. Tell him his daughter—she will speak to him." Rivkah's English was awkward and heavily accented, but her meaning was all too clear.

Emily expected Daddy wouldn't waste any time answering this kind of call, and she was right. Not ten seconds later Rivkah was making her demands again.

"Yes, I have Emily here, Major Porkinson...Parkinson. What? Yes, she's fine—for now. No, you listen. I'm in charge now, and I tell you what to do. You have fifteen minutes to agree to demands! If not, you never see daughter again!" Rivkah nearly shouted the words. She turned her back to Emily and started pacing once more, another cloud of smoke rising over her head.

"Yes, I *know* he told you four o'clock. That's not good enough anymore. Deadline has been moved up now. Fifteen minutes. No missed deadline! We speak directly now." Rivkah paused, listening.

"Your daughter? She's here." She paused again, then sighed. "A few words only."

EMILY'S PLAN

The Arab man leading his two mules over the ridge of the hill looked as surprised to see Dov and the Americans as they were to see him. He was draped in a flowing robe, more than roomy enough to hide a rifle, topped by a black-striped kaffiyeh. He stopped to look them over, and his dark eyes danced as if someone had just told him a joke.

"Hello?" Stan stepped out into the road to meet him. "We're on our way to Ashkelon, and—"

"We need to offer him something," whispered Chip. "Quickly!" He found a bag of figs in the car, saved for a traveling snack, and passed them to the Arab man.

"Does he speak English?" Clarence asked.

The Arab man looked up. "English? Sure! Cheerio. Lucky Strike. A-OK." He gave them a thumbs-up sign. So far, so good.

The man's two mules swatted flies with their tails as they waited on the road behind their master. He had crouched with his back to the wreck, enjoying the figs and appearing in no particular hurry.

Dov glanced over his shoulder at the way they had come. This man surely didn't have anything to do with the attack.

"Ditch is bigger than you think, eh?" So he *did* speak a little English. He laughed as he looked over the Model A. But his smile slipped away when he held up a piece of the ruined tire in his hand.

"Flat tire." Stan raised his voice and talked very slowly. He started to act out what had happened, but the others shushed him.

"That I see." The Arab put his finger in a small splintered hole in the side of the car, one of the bullet holes. He turned to face them with a question on his face. "But who shoots at you?"

The Americans looked at one another. No one seemed to think it was a good idea to explain everything to this man, but Dov could tell he already knew the answer.

"Azzam is not a fool!" the man thundered. "He sees what has happened. It is not our way to shoot at guests! Not good at all."

Dov tried to back out of the man's way, but Azzam grabbed his arm before he could get away. "Now, boy, I help you. You help me first. Give me rope."

Dov looked around. He had been volunteered and wasn't sure why, but there it was. Stan gave him the rope, and Dov helped run the end of the towline to the mule team.

"Now, you push ..." Their rescuer pointed to Stan and Chip. "And the rest, you pull. We all pull together and get your car out of ditch, eh?"

So that's what they did, after Azzam whispered something into the ears of his mules. It must have worked, as the two animals grunted and pulled harder than any of them.

"It's coming!" yelled Stan as the Model A scraped and rolled out of the ditch. A minute later they all clapped to see their car was free.

"There, you see?" When Azzam smiled Dov could count three gold teeth. "Not all Arabs crazy with rifles. You be more careful after now."

No one seemed to mind that Azzam took the rest of their figs with him. He popped another in his mouth as he waved good-bye.

"Let's get this new tire on and get going!" Stan clapped his hands, and they all hurried to help. Azzam turned back just in time to catch Dov's eye. "Go home, you tell your President Truman that Azzam helped you."

Dov nodded, but he didn't have the heart to tell this man he wasn't even sure who President Truman was. Right now he was more worried about reaching Ashkelon before anything else happened.

✡ ✡ ✡

"All right, we're here." Stan rested his hands on the steering wheel and looked out at the main street in front of them. They could see that Ashkelon was just like its picture on postcards, with hills behind them to the east and the blue Mediterranean not far away in the opposite direction. Ahead of them stretched the dusty main street, bordered by twin rows of sleepy concrete storefronts. A group of men sitting in front of one of the stores gave them a curious look. Maybe they weren't used to seeing groups of American college students touring through their town. Certainly not in the past few years.

"The good news is that Ashkelon looks like a small place." Chip glanced up from his road map and peered around. "Maybe someone could direct us?"

"Yeah, we'll just knock on everyone's doors and ask for an English girl," Les joked.

No one laughed.

"I was only joking," added Les.

"Unless someone has a better idea . . ." Stan looked around at the group. "Emily Parkinson is a prisoner somewhere in this town. It might take us a while, but who else is going to help her if we don't?"

"And what do we *do* when we find her?" Clarence asked what Dov had been wondering all along.

"We'll cross that bridge when we come to it," Stan decided.

Dov could see as well as anyone else what they had to do. He climbed out and knocked on the door of the first building he saw.

"Be careful, now," Stan warned them as they fanned out. He stayed in the car, idling slowly down the street.

✡ ✡ ✡

Rivkah held the receiver to her chest and turned to give Emily a dagger expression. "One wrong word, girl, and I'll personally see to it that you never see your parents again. You will not try anything clever. No messages. Do we understand each other?"

Emily nodded seriously.

"Say hello to your father," Rivkah commanded. "Tell him you are fine. Nothing more, nothing less. Understand?"

Emily nodded again. She supposed it was better for her to talk to her father than for someone else to do it. But it felt like years since she had seen him.

Rivkah held out the receiver and nodded her go-ahead.

"Daddy!" The sound of her own hoarse whisper nearly

scared Emily.

Rivkah signaled her to say more, but it would not be that easy, not through her tears.

"I'm ..." Emily tried to choke the words out, but they would not come.

"Princess, is that you?" Emily's father sounded far away. "Are you all right?"

"I . . . I'm all right. I miss you. . . ."

"There." Rivkah took charge of the receiver, bringing it back to her own ear. "You hear that? Your daughter, she is fine. If you want her to stay fine, you meet our demands. Fifteen minutes!"

Rivkah barked out the phone number, slammed the receiver down with a chuckle, then gasped when she heard a knock at the front door behind her.

"Rivkah!" came Levi's muffled voice. "Open up."

Emily's captor turned to her with a fierce expression in her eyes. "Not a word to Levi about this," she hissed. "And perhaps I'll let you speak with your daddy again."

This time Emily didn't nod. She didn't believe a word Rivkah told her. Would they keep their word to release her if her father was able to free the criminal from Acre Prison? What would happen if Yehuda wasn't set free? If Daddy couldn't meet their demands? She shivered at the thought.

Levi pounded on the door. *Why doesn't Levi just come in the back door?* wondered Emily. The thought gave her an idea. That and all the noise still coming from the street.

Levi pounded on the door as if his life depended on it.

"I'm coming, I'm coming!" Rivkah rolled her eyes and shook her head as she fished for another cigarette under a pile of newspapers on the kitchen table. It was a wonder she hadn't started a fire yet.

Emily didn't sit still. As soon as Rivkah turned her back, she gathered her strength, tilted forward onto her feet, and backed her way quietly around to the front side of the kitchen table, the side closest to the front door. Only a few feet separated them.

"Will you wait just a minute?" Rivkah whined, pausing to light a match before reaching the door.

Emily felt like a bee aiming her stinger as she peered over her shoulder and pointed the feet of her chair at Rivkah and the front door.

✡ ✡ ✡

"Have you seen an English girl?"

By now all the Americans were well into the search with Dov. They ran from door to door of the town center, asking women in the shops, men sitting in the sun. Has anyone seen an English girl? The answer was always the same: a shrug, a shake of the head. No one had any idea what these odd visitors were talking about.

"Keep going!" Stan coached them in the car as he idled slowly down the center of the main street. "She has to be on this street somewhere. We've checked everywhere else."

Stan hadn't told them what to do when they found her—if they found her. After all, was there really much chance the kidnappers would answer their door and invite these strangers in for a chat? How do you do? Tea in the garden? No doubt the kidnappers would be overjoyed to see them.

What other choice do we have? Dov thought. They were on a crusade. And Dov had the oddest feeling that if Emily *was* being hidden anywhere in dusty Ashkelon, they were going to find her.

How could he be so sure? Maybe it was the way the Americans had prayed—not just before eating or sleeping, but the entire time in the car. And Dov had by now decided that if anyone could talk to God, they could. He had tagged along with them in their prayers, as if dipping his toe into a swimming hole when he still didn't know how to swim. But he was convinced that if God had an idea to listen to anyone, He would listen to these kindhearted Americans.

But there was no time to think more about the Americans and their prayers. Dov led the charge down the street, past surprised housewives clutching bags of groceries, bundles of cucumbers and squash.

"English girl?" asked a shopkeeper wiping his hands on a smudged blue apron. "In Ashkelon—and alone? Maybe Jerusalem or Tel Aviv, but not Ashkelon. No English here."

Finally Stan stopped the car at the end of the street.

"I don't think she's here." Chip scratched his head and stood next to the Ford while the others gathered around. Stan looked to Les and Clarence, both of them sweating and looking beat. They shook their heads, too, and Stan rested his forehead against his steering wheel.

"We tried, Dov."

"I know."

DESPERATE ATTEMPT

The click of the opening door was Emily's signal to move. As Levi began to step inside, she aimed her chair and pushed backward for the door as fast and as hard as she could.

"Something's going on out here. The street's full of—" Levi didn't get a chance to finish when Emily slammed into him full force with her battering-ram chair.

"What are you—" Rivkah shrieked in protest.

Levi couldn't step out of the way fast enough, or maybe he didn't know what hit him.

In her backward rush, Emily hadn't been able to see a thing, of course, but that hadn't kept her from backpedaling with all her strength. She felt the chair legs crack; then she tumbled backward over Rivkah.

Levi found his voice, yelping as Emily bounced and then came down hard on his leg with the solid wooden seat of the chair. Emily hadn't planned it that way, but she didn't mind putting all her weight down in one place.

If they recaptured her, what then? Emily had already decided it couldn't be worse than what she already faced. For an instant she thought of what Dov must have felt during his time in the Nazi death camps. Hers was a small taste, perhaps, but real enough. She kicked and rolled and found herself blinking in the sunlight on the hard-packed dirt road—away from the tangle of Levi's and Rivkah's arms and legs.

Now that the chair had broken, she could stand. Her hands, though, were still bound tightly behind her. Rivkah had made sure of that.

No, she couldn't expect to outrun Levi and Rivkah. But she could scream! And as Emily stumbled into the street, she let loose an awful, wonderful shriek.

By the end of their search, Dov and the Americans had noticed only four British soldiers in town. The uniformed men stood about a half block away, casually checking cars and slowing traffic. A typical military checkpoint.

But Dov knew something was different when an Arab man pointed their direction, and the four soldiers wasted no time hurrying toward them. That might have been all right, except these soldiers would ask him the same questions other Jews were asked: Who are you? Where did you come from? Where are your papers? Right now, those were questions Dov was not ready to answer.

He looked to the opposite end of the street when he heard a crash and a shout—like the sounds of a fight, or a troublemaker being thrown out of a store. But then came the screams.

One look told him it wasn't a brawl. About a block away, in the direction they had just come from, Dov could clearly see a girl struggling to her feet in the dirt. The remnants of a chair were scattered in the street near her. The dark-haired girl stumbled a few steps as a man and a woman struggled to their feet behind her.

The man bellowed like a wild boar. It was obvious he would do some serious damage to the runaway when he caught up with her.

But the runaway—there was something about her. . . .

"It's *her*!" Dov shouted to the others. "Down the street!"

Stan and the others looked to see what Dov was shouting about. So did everyone else on the street—the shoppers, the old men, the British soldiers. Farther down the block in the opposite direction from Emily, the soldiers were picking up speed as they trotted toward the Model A.

Dov hopped onto the running board, just outside the car doors, and again pointed.

"Falling into the street—it's Emily."

"Are you sure?" Stan asked, but one look at Dov seemed to convince him.

"That's it, then." Stan waved at his crew from the driver's seat. "Get in, everyone!"

Chip dove in, with Les and Clarence right behind him. Dov clung to the door as the North Philadelphia Young All-Church Council Holyland '47 Goodwill Tour picked up speed.

But Dov was afraid they wouldn't be able to reach her in time. Her captors were only a half dozen steps behind her, and she obviously wasn't going to win any footraces with her arms still tied up.

"Faster!" Dov urged the car and its driver on, the way he would a stubborn mule out for a slow trot. Behind him the young British soldiers were catching up. One of them blew a shrill whistle. What did they know?

"Hold up, there!" yelled a man in uniform. They were almost as close behind the Model A as the man up ahead was to Emily.

"Stan?" Chip looked behind them. "Shouldn't we stop?"

"Emily!" Dov hollered.

Emily looked at them with wide eyes; so did her kidnappers. But Dov wasn't about to stay for introductions, especially not considering the whistle-blowing soldiers on their heels. He would have to get it right the first time, because Stan obviously had no intention of slowing down.

"Can you do it?" Stan shouted.

Dov nodded and held on tight. He wasn't going to get much help from Emily, not with her hands tied behind her back. He got ready to scoop her up off the street with his free left arm.

Emily must have seen what he was trying to do; she stumbled and quickened her step. Dov felt one of the Americans grip him around the waist, freeing both his arms. Just when the man behind Emily was about to grab her, Dov reached out as far as he could. Emily launched herself into his arms.

✡ ✡ ✡

"Naturally I'm grateful to you, but ..." Emily searched for the right words. "But I still don't understand. Why didn't you give me back to the English soldiers when you had a chance? And why did you help me in the first place?"

"The folks at Yad Shalom are already in enough trouble as it is," Stan replied, his jaw set firmly as he drove. "I don't know if we did the right thing, but we just wanted to get you back to your folks as quickly as possible without getting anybody else in trouble, like Dov here."

Emily knew what Stan was talking about. She rested the back of her head on the seat as they bounced up the highway. At last she was free, driving in the direction of home. Only one thing was left to do: get home, and get home soon. Especially so Daddy would know not to release the terrorist prisoner.

The late afternoon sun dropped behind them, casting a long shadow on the road ahead. Emily listened to the Americans tell and retell their story, each filling in a bit here, a piece there.

Dov, on the other hand, sat stone silent, staring out the window. His part in the rescue she still didn't understand.

"Dov?" She tried to catch his eye, but it was no use.

He hugged the door, shrugged his shoulders. "It was *their* idea. The Americans needed something to write home about, if you want to know."

Stan and the others laughed, but Emily was sure Dov had not been trying to make a joke.

"A lesson in peace," added Chip. "That's what we came here for, isn't it?"

"Peace?" Dov looked as if he almost choked. "I don't think Eretz Israel is a good place to learn peace."

"It's the places that need peace that are the best for learning it," said Stan. "We're glad we came, but it was your friend Dov here who wanted to help you more than anyone else. After all, we'd never met you."

Dov looked as if he was fascinated by the rolling hills and ravines of the desert landscape building up to Jerusalem.

"Is that true?" Emily wanted to know. She *had* to know.

No one spoke; the car was quiet for a few minutes.

"I was just paying you back the favor," Dov finally admitted. "You pulled me out of the water and saved me from drowning. So I pulled you off the street. A favor for a favor. Now we're even."

"But you came looking for me. You saved my life," Emily objected. "I insist on repaying you."

"No." Dov sighed. "No more paying and repaying. You

repay me by not repaying me. We're even."

"Now, now." Stan tried to referee.

"Here." Emily picked up Chip's notebook, jotted down her address, and tore off the sheet of paper. "This is where I live in Jerusalem. You have no place to stay, and my father could help you."

But when she tried to hand it to Dov, he only pushed it back.

"Your father?" He glared at her. Dov tried again to wave the note away, but Emily showed him that she could be stubborn, too.

"Your father is the kind of man who would put me in prison," he muttered. "If he could, he would send me back to Poland. You said so yourself. . . ."

Emily closed her eyes and let the warm wind blow through her hair. What could she say to him?

"Dov, I'm so sorry for all the horrible things I said back at the kibbutz about turning you in to the authorities. I was wrong. I didn't mean them, and I shouldn't have been so cruel. But my father is really quite fair. I daresay he *would* help you."

For a moment, just a moment, Dov looked as if he was thinking of the idea. Who better to help him find his family than a British major? He even held the address in his hand for a moment—before crumpling it. But then his face clouded over, and Emily knew it would never happen.

Try as she might, she couldn't contain her frustration.

"Honestly! Just let me help you. Why must you be such a twit?"

"There you go again, calling me names. I don't ask for your help, but you push it at me. Don't you understand?"

"I understand that you're proud and pigheaded."

"And now you insult me!"

"Dov, if you'd only—"

"All right, kids. We're not out of the woods yet." Stan pointed at a checkpoint up ahead. He hit the steering wheel with his hands. "I should have known we would be stopped."

ROADBLOCK

17

Emily's heart leaped at the sight of the British roadblock up ahead. Without thinking, she smiled. Surely these soldiers would recognize her. They would believe her about her father, of course, especially after she told them about Levi and Rivkah. And they would make sure word reached Major Parkinson right away.

"Do you think the soldiers back in Ashkelon might have radioed ahead about us?" Chip asked.

Emily hadn't thought about that. She understood the Americans were caught in the middle. They wanted to help her, but they didn't want to get Dov and the kibbutz in trouble, either.

"If they did," Stan replied, "we have nothing to hide, except ..."

"Except me." Dov finished Stan's sentence and slouched lower in his seat.

Emily looked over at her stubborn friend and tried to imagine what he was thinking—if that was possible. Perhaps he meant well enough—he *had* rescued her, after all. What would happen to him?

She counted three soldiers up ahead, stopping and checking every car that passed by. Their jeep was parked sideways, blocking traffic going east into Jerusalem.

"Can't we stop and let Dov out?" asked Clarence.

"Too late." Chip shook his head no. "They've already seen us."

Emily bit her lip and made up her mind. "I've got an idea."

✡ ✡ ✡

The plan was simple, really. Dov understood it gave him three, maybe four minutes to run to the top of the hill next to the road and disappear. Of course, if he got caught, that was another matter. It wasn't quite dark yet. His stomach tied itself into a knot as he crouched on the floorboards.

"We picked up this girl on the street," announced Stan when they pulled up to where the three soldiers waited. "She said she was kidnapped."

Emily didn't wait to be asked; she jumped out of the car as if she had just found a long-lost relative.

"Oh, this is marvelous. I'm *so* glad you stopped us!" she cried. It sounded good from where Dov was hiding. "I'm Emily Parkinson—my father is Major Parkinson—and these kind people...saved me...from ..."

That was his signal.

Chip clapped him on the shoulder. "There she goes," the American whispered. "She's fainting, right on schedule."

Dov nodded and crawled out the open back door on all fours.

"Remember," Chip whispered, "just two miles that way, over the hill. Shalom."

Dov looked over his shoulder at the people in the Model A. *Shalom. Peace.*

"Thank you," he whispered back. "And . . ." Why was it so hard to say? ". . . and tell Emily thank you."

Chip shooed him off with a grin. Dov scrambled over the edge of the pavement into a ditch and away from the road before another car came up behind them. He figured he had about three minutes at most while all the soldiers were distracted with trying to help Emily. Three minutes to disappear.

It didn't really matter which way he went, as long as it was away—and fast. He half crawled, half ran, trying always to stay low. He waited to hear a shout, someone ordering him to "Halt!" Or maybe a shot. He kept his head down, running, falling in the rocks, getting up.

The safest route would be to run around the base of the hill, sideways and up, until he was out of sight. Faster would be to run straight up the side of the hill, though if he did, he would be out in plain daylight for all to see. Dov took the chance and headed straight up.

The hill was rockier than he'd thought. Slippery with loose, sandy rock, almost treacherous in places. But he scrambled ahead, afraid to look back, panic taking over. *Run!* He ran faster than he ever had before until he lost his footing and tumbled feetfirst between two boulders.

"Oh!" Dov gasped at the pain that suddenly gripped and twisted his leg. Five steps from the top of the hill and freedom and he had skinned the side of his knee clean! Worse yet, he'd sent a cascade of head-sized rocks tumbling back down the hill, right at the roadblock!

✡ ✡ ✡

Emily smiled inwardly, satisfied her grand performance had worked.

We did it!

She thought of Dov, climbing over the top of the hill on his way to Jerusalem, and she wondered if she would see him again. Probably not. But she whispered a prayer for him anyway.

Please help him find his family, she prayed silently. *Please help him find peace. . . .*

"She's coming to!" said one of the young soldiers.

"Here, miss, some water." Another soldier helped her sit up. The third young man had produced a tin cup and was pouring water from a canteen for her. It was warm and tasted of metal, but she couldn't say no. She smiled and took a sip. The Americans had gathered around, too, forming a ring around the three soldiers.

"She's been through a lot," Stan said. "We tried to help her, but—"

"Yes, well, you've done the right thing," said the soldier with the canteen. "I just heard a report about the kidnapping. Won't the major be glad to hear we've rescued his daughter."

"Yes, quite." Emily smiled. "Quite gallant, er, Private . . ."

"Burrows." The soldier straightened up. "John Burrows."

"Private Burrows. I'll be certain to mention you to my father." And she would; he seemed a nice enough young man.

One of the other soldiers suddenly straightened up and looked around. "Did someone shout?" He glanced up at the hillside to the right of the road, and his eyes grew wide.

"Rockslide!" he cried.

✡ ✡ ✡

Dov watched with horror as the rocks tumbled down at his friends. After he'd yelled his warning, he crouched down behind the biggest rock, almost out of sight.

Please, no!

Thump, thump— Dov peeked out through his hands to see the largest rocks in the avalanche bounce in a wide arc to the left, well behind the cars. Some smashed to pebbles when they hit the road; others danced to the far side. The people below were scrambling, but they were obviously out of danger.

He sighed with relief. "Sorry about that," he whispered.

But now the soldiers were pointing his way, and he stiffened once more with fright. They must have wondered what started the avalanche. Did they see him hiding? It was only five steps to the top of the hill. Should he run for it?

No, he wasn't sure he could make it, even if he wanted to. The throbbing in his knee reminded him of the mess he was now in. For the moment he was trapped. At least the soldiers weren't coming up after him. Not yet.

Dov decided he should probably wait a few hours for night to fall, then try his knee again. But the thought of waiting and risking discovery …

A torn strip from his shirt worked as a temporary bandage to slow the bleeding.

Enough! Dov wasn't going to wait. *Let them shoot me.*

He tried his knee; it hurt but moved. With a deep breath he started forward, not daring to look back.

✡ ✡ ✡

Two hours later Dov was still walking—or hobbling. He'd followed a trail through the barren hills, grateful the soldiers hadn't chased him after all. Sometimes the trail seemed not much wider than a goat track, sometimes as wide as a jeep road. Like the hills around him, it was rugged and led up and down, but mostly up, the way he wanted to go. Up to Zion. Dov knew he would be there soon, maybe before sundown.

On the way he thought about Moshe and his offer. Moshe was serious, he knew, about making a homeland for Jews in this place. Dov liked the idea of having a country he could call home, but not the way Moshe was trying to make it happen.

And what about Henrik and his peace rebel ideas, and the Americans who had thrown themselves into danger for someone they didn't even know? He had to admit that he liked them and Henrik. Liked them a lot. Already he missed them. Why, he even missed ... But no, he didn't want to think about Emily.

Keep your mind on the trail. Another step closer to Jerusalem. He wiped the sweat from his forehead and checked his knee. A little messy, but it would mend. At least this trip would not be as far as his trek over the Alps into Italy.

He could almost feel Jerusalem getting closer, as if he were sailing through the fog, closing in on a lighthouse. Between the hills, he passed from blue shadows to the last light of the day as the sun slowly sank behind him. Almost there.

Then Dov heard them—explosions, one after the other. Muffled *booms* up ahead where he knew the city waited for him. Dov hurried his steps, trying to ignore the stiffness settling into his knee, trying his best not to fall. The sound echoed through the hills, then echoed again, and then the only thing he heard was his own heavy breathing and far-off human cries.

What's that? Dov stopped to listen. The mournful sounds sent shivers up his spine.

He pushed himself to the top of the next ridge, where he could finally see the city spread out above him. He gasped at the sight.

Jerusalem. The City of Peace.

Just then, though, it looked like anything but. Ugly black smoke rose to the sky as explosions rumbled once more.

But still, what a city! He'd never seen such a collection of grand stone buildings, church steeples, tall Muslim minaret towers, domes, ancient walls...and all in a warm pink stone that seemed to glow in the setting sun. The welcome would have been perfect, if not for the...bombs?

Stop crying! he told himself. But what else could he do at the sight of the place he'd traveled so far to see? He caught his breath and watched and listened.

Another sad cry pierced the twilight. A call to peace? Or a call to prayer?

"Thank you," Dov finally whispered a prayer, and the words surprised him. But it was the only thing he could think of to say to the One who had brought him so far.

THE ALIYAH BET

If Emily and Dov had been able to listen to the radio as they drove the road to Jerusalem*, they might have heard the big news: In a matter of weeks the United Nations was preparing to vote on a partition plan for Palestine. *Partition* means to *divide up*, and that was exactly the problem. As the British prepared to leave Palestine for good, they were desperately looking for a plan to make everyone happy, a way they could divide up the land into neat Jewish and Arab sections.

They couldn't do it. No one ever came up with a plan that everyone liked. But most of the UN proposals would give the Jews a small homeland, and some Arabs were upset that the Jews would be given any territory at all.

That's the argument Emily and Dov stepped into when they reached Eretz Israel, the Land of Israel. No one seemed to trust anyone else, and all were afraid that the land they claimed would be taken away. The same arguments continue today!

The pressures of living in such a country were even worse for Dov, who was part of the *Aliyah Bet*, the illegal immigration. *Aliyah* means *going up* in Hebrew, as in "going up to the Promised Land." Dov quickly discovered what that meant when he climbed the steep hills around Jerusalem. And *bet* is the second letter of the Hebrew alphabet. So Aliyah Bet was sort of like a *second* way of immigrating—sneaking into the country.

Many details in this adventure are lifted straight from the history books. A few illegal Aliyah Bet immigrants *did* manage to slip ashore past the British guards. And Jews of all kinds came to escape war-torn Europe—including families, orphans, and lone survivors. Often they were helped by Israeli agents to hide and blend into the country, just as it happened in this book. Sometimes members of Jewish collective farms, or kibbutzes, took in illegal immigrants, too.

At that time, one of those kibbutzes (*kibbutzim* in Hebrew) was called *Yad Mordecai*, and our description of life on the Yad Shalom kibbutz was inspired by real experiences in that place.

In 1947 tensions were high between Arabs and Jews no matter where one lived. It was tense in the villages, tense in the cities, tense on the roads. The Arabs thought the Jews were going to take over all of their land. The Jews thought they had a right to their homeland, and that the Arabs would attack at any time. Many people on both sides were ready to fight, and it was very dangerous to travel about the country.

That's why it was unusual for a group of young Americans to visit that year. But the group from Philadelphia in this book is based on an actual group of young tourists who traveled Palestine during that time.

One other part of this book needs more explanation. There have never been a large number of Jews who believe in the Peace Rebel of our title, the Messiah Jesus. But the number is growing all the time. And for people like Henrik, Matthias, and Dov, the incredible adventures are only just beginning.

*By the way, in case you're wondering why Emily and Dov didn't listen to the news in their Model A Ford, well, that car was built in 1929 and didn't come with a radio. Most cars didn't have radios until the 1940s.

FROM THE AUTHOR

The adventures don't stop with the last page of this book! Here are five great ideas for you to try:

1. *Jump into the next adventure*, the third in our PROMISE OF ZION series. Check out the preview on page 158.

2. *Discover other books.* I've put together a list of some of my favorite books, magazines, Web sites, music, and more on Israel. They'll help you get a better feel for the strange and wonderful land that became Emily and Dov's home. Be sure to show this section to your parents or teacher.

3. *Write to me.* I always enjoy hearing from readers, and I answer all my mail. (Or as Emily would say, my post.) How did you like the book? Do you have a question about anything that happened, or about what the characters were thinking? What's next? My address is: Bethany House Publishers, 11400 Hampshire Avenue South, Minneapolis, MN, USA 55438.

4. *Subscribe to my newsletter*, called *Write Now!* It includes things like writing tips, the "inside scoop" on the latest book, or funny behind-the-scenes stories. If you want a copy, just send a stamped, self-addressed envelope to me at my Bethany House address (see number 3). Be sure to include a note explaining that you want Robert Elmer's newsletter.

5. *Go online.* Visit my Web site at www.coolreading.com. That's where you can pick up writing tips from your favorite authors,

share your ideas online, or even review a book. There's plenty of cool stuff to do at coolreading. Check out my bulletin board for the latest news, too.

That should keep you busy…until the next adventure.

Blessings!

WANT TO KNOW MORE?

You're in luck! The library, bookstands, and even the Internet are full of great resources for learning more about Israel and about the incredible events that happened there between 1946 and 1949. Here are a few ideas to get you started.

Picture Books on Israel

• *The Bible Lands Holyland Journey* by Dr. Randall D. Smith. Published by Doko in Israel, this is one of the better picture books of Israel and the Holy Land I've found. You'll see pictures of many of the places Dov and Emily visit.

History

• *Dawn of the Promised Land* by Ben Wicks (Hyperion 1997). This book was written for Israel's fiftieth anniversary, and it's very good. It's not exactly a children's book, but there are lots of really interesting interviews with people remembering what it was like to be a kid in 1948, doing the kinds of things Dov and Emily did.

• *Zvi* by Elwood McQuaid. Zvi Kalisher's story inspired many of the events in Dov Zalinski's life. In fact, I had a chance to interview him personally in his Jerusalem home. The book is available through the Friends of Israel Gospel Ministry in New Jersey. (PO Box 908, Bellmawr, NJ 08099). They also have an interesting magazine called *Israel, My Glory*.

• *The Creation of Israel* by Linda Jacobs Altman (Lucent Books

World History Series 1998). A good all-in-one history of how Israel was founded, with a timeline, index, and pictures. A perfect resource for writing a research paper.

• *Child of the Warsaw Ghetto* by David Adler, illustrated by Karen Ritz. Some of the scenes in this picture book are sad and difficult to look at, but it shows what people like Dov went through during the worst days of World War II.

Hebrew

• *Hebrew for Everyone*, published and distributed by Epistle. Here's a fun, kid-friendly approach to learning the language of the Old Testament—and today's Israel! The study guide is written by Hebrew believers in Jesus, and is designed for kids and beginners. You can even learn the Lord's Prayer in Hebrew! I picked up my copy at the Garden Tomb in Jerusalem for twenty shekels. (A shekel is about twenty-five cents.) Contact Epistle at PO Box 2817, Petach Tikva, 49127, Israel.

Internet Sites

• International Christian Embassy, Jerusalem (www.icej.org.il) is a good place to start for all kinds of links to travel and historic information on Jerusalem and Israel.

• U.S. Holocaust Memorial Museum (www.ushmm.org). This is the leading museum in North America for information on what happened to the Jewish people before, during, and after World War II.

• Station Wagons on the Web. For a picture of the kind of Model A Ford that Dov and his American friends rode in, go to www.stationwagon.com/gallery/1929_Ford_Model_A.html.

Music

• *Adonai: The Power of Worship From the Land of Israel* (Integrity Music). Besides some lively worship tunes with Hebrew and English words, this CD also has a brief historic audio clip from 1948. It's produced and performed by Jewish believers, and I often put it on for inspiration during the writing of this book!

PREVIEW

History is about to explode in book three of
PROMISE OF ZION, *Refugee Treasure*.

When Dov finally makes it to Jerusalem, the city is a war zone—and he can't find his family! He makes friends with an old Arab shopkeeper, but finds out the hard way that Jews and Arabs aren't *supposed* to be friends. And what about the men in the street who are always watching the shop? Why are they so interested in ancient scrolls? Emily tries to help, but at first it only seems to make matters worse. And then Dov discovers a secret back-room entry to a maze of underground tunnels…which lead to more danger than anyone could imagine!

THE YOUNG UNDERGROUND—
a "prequel" to PROMISE OF ZION!

On a black night in Denmark, evil prowled the streets. . . .

If you liked this PROMISE OF ZION book, you're sure to enjoy THE YOUNG UNDERGROUND. In the opening to these eight exciting adventures, eleven-year-old Peter Andersen and his sister, Elise, help their Jewish friend Henrik escape the Nazis in World War II Denmark. But it doesn't stop there! Find out what happened to some of the PROMISE OF ZION characters during their early years.

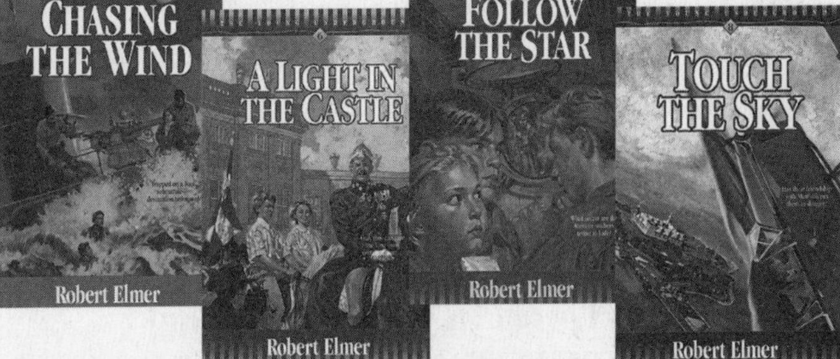